Dancing for the Devil
Part Two:

Blue Bonnets

Marie Laval

Published by Accent Press Ltd 2016

ISBN 9781783758692

Rose Saintclair's tale begins in *The Dream Catcher*, the first part of the **Dancing for the Devil** trilogy.

The story so far…

Cape Wrath, Scotland, November 1847.

Rose is travelling to meet her new husband when her ship is caught in a terrifying storm off the far north of Scotland. Her first glimpse of Wrath Lodge, makes Rose think of the gateway to hell and her encounter with Wrath's laird Bruce McGunn does nothing to reassure her. A reckless officer discharged from the army, McGunn holds a bitter grudge against her husband's family, the wealthy McRaes, and Rose is soon horrified to find out that he means to hold her to ransom in order to save his estate from financial ruin.

Bruce's health is failing and, with terrifying hallucinations tormenting him every night, he fears he is descending into madness. Soon other things are keeping him awake – a growing attraction for his feisty and exotic captive, and the gruesome discovery of two women's bodies washed ashore near the castle. One of them, Rose's childhood friend Malika, she last saw in Algiers the day before her marriage to McRae. How the women died, who killed them and disposed of their bodies is a mystery Bruce now has to solve.

Determined not to miss the ball where her darling Cameron promised to announce their secret wedding, Rose manages to escape dark, gloomy Wrath. She takes with her a posy of pine sprigs she believes was given to her by the Dark Lady, Wrath's resident ghost, and confused feelings for Wrath's brutal and tormented master – the man she calls *McGlum*...

Chapter One

'You think I was doing what?' Bruce shot Kilroy a disbelieving glance.

The doctor shuffled his papers and piled them up in a precarious pyramid on his desk.

'Sleepwalking,' he answered without looking up. 'How else can you explain what happened last night? You said yourself you couldn't remember much.'

Bruce shook his head.

'Maybe I wasn't the one sleepwalking.'

He took a deep breath and raked his fingers in his hair. 'The thing is, it's happened before, with Rose McRae I mean.'

This time, Kilroy looked up.

'You mean she's already been in your room in the middle of the night?'

Bruce smiled. 'Actually, she was in my bed the night she arrived.'

Kilroy sat down heavily on his padded leather chair, folded his hands on his stomach, and narrowed his eyes.

'You got her into bed the very first night? You work fast, my friend. I'm glad to see the old "claymore devil" hasn't lost any of his sharp edges.'

Bruce shook his head. 'It wasn't like that. I mean, I didn't…we didn't… She kind of stumbled into it.'

Kilroy chuckled. 'How can she stumble into your bed when your room is up a tower at the other end of the Lodge?'

Bruce didn't answer but turned and pressed his forehead against the cool window pane. He had spent the whole afternoon at Morag's bedside and hadn't even noticed how late it was. It was evening now, and people would be rushing home

1

or pushing the door to the Old Norse's Inn for a quiet pint of ale or a game of dominoes near the peat fire.

'She was chasing after a ghost,' Bruce said in a low voice.

'What ghost? You talk in riddles, McGunn.'

Bruce sighed and turned to face his friend. 'It doesn't matter. Anyway, I don't sleepwalk. I would know if I did it, after years bivouacking and sleeping in army barracks.'

'You may have only just started doing it. The unusual symptoms you've experienced lately, the memory loss, nightmares and vivid dreams you mentioned, all go hand in hand with sleepwalking.'

'But don't worry,' Kilroy added quickly, 'somnambulism isn't that serious. The trick is to prevent you from getting injured. From now on, you must lock your door or put some piece of furniture to block your stairs at night to make sure you don't wander on, or off, the cliff.'

'I'll soon have more pressing things to worry me than the need to drag cupboards across my staircase,' Bruce retorted grimly. 'I have bankers and their bailiffs to ward off, a killer to catch, and I may have a duel on my hands before long – if McRae is brave enough to face me.'

Kilroy cocked his eyebrow. 'A duel?'

Bruce drew in a deep, long breath.

'Half my household saw Rose McRae asleep in my arms this morning.'

'Ah. That's unfortunate.'

'Unfortunate? It's a bloody disaster!' Bruce thundered. 'The woman doesn't remember a thing. She has no idea her reputation is – or will soon be – in tatters and her husband may cast her off for adultery. How the hell do I tell her?'

Kilroy toyed with a bronze letter-opener.

'Maybe you won't have to. Maybe your people won't talk. With the bad weather coming our way again, there won't be much travelling between here and Thurso or Westmore in the next few days.'

'You know as well as I do that the weather won't stop tongues from wagging. Gossip always finds a way, especially that kind of gossip.'

2

Kilroy stabbed a pile of letters with his letter-opener. 'You may be right. I wonder...'

He paused and reclined on the back of his seat.

'It does strike me as odd that neither of you remember much about last night. It's as if you were both struck by some kind of amnesia.'

'Perhaps it was the curse of the Northern Lights,' Bruce replied with a shrug. 'It's late. I'd better go,' he went on. 'Are you sure Morag is going to be all right tonight? She seems very weak.'

The woman had clutched at his hand, refusing to let him leave her side and asking for forgiveness again and again. Every time he asked what he should forgive, she'd turned her head to the wall without answering.

Kilroy stood up. 'Her heart is in bad shape and she is frail, but for now she'll be comfortable enough in my spare room. Don't worry. I'll keep an eye on her throughout the night.'

'Thanks, Kilroy.'

Bruce slipped his riding coat on and walked to the front door.

'How long before you travel to Westmore?' Kilroy asked.

'Two or three days, at most.'

Kilroy swayed back and forth on the balls of his feet, and coughed to clear his throat.

'I hope that what MacBoyd was telling me last night in the public house isn't true.'

'What was that?'

The doctor leant closer and lowered his voice. 'That you intend to keep Rose McRae here as some kind of guarantee against her husband and his business associates.'

Bruce silently promised to give MacBoyd a terse telling off. He had no right talking to Kilroy, or anyone else, about his plans.

'What I'm doing with Lady McRae is nobody's business, not even yours.'

Shock registered on the doctor's face.

'So it's true! And I thought McBoyd had had too much ale. These aren't the old days of the clan wars, McGunn. You can't keep a woman locked up in your tower and hold her to ransom.'

'I'll do what I must to protect my estate and my people against McRae and his bankers. Not that I have to justify myself to you.'

Kilroy looked sharply at McGunn but he must have thought better than to insist because he shook his head and added with a resigned smile, 'Well, you know best, I suppose.'

He opened the door. Bruce stepped outside and breathed in a lungful of icy wind. There was more snow on the way but for now the half, butter-yellow moon played hide and seek with black clouds.

'I'll drop by in the morning to check on Morag.'

The two men shook hands and Bruce made his way to the stables behind Kilroy's house. A short while later he was riding back to Wrath Lodge, the man and the horse darker than the night on the deserted cliff path.

The loud sounding of the horn woke Rose with a start and she bumped her head against the side panel inside the coach.

'By Old Ibrahim's Beard, what was that terrible racket?' she gasped, rubbing the forehead with her fingers.

'Only the post-guard warning the coaching inn of our arrival. We're stopping for the night,' the man sitting next to her replied.

As the carriage lurched around a bend in the road, he shifted on the seat and Rose caught wafts of wet dog from his pelisse and horse manure from his boots. Queasy once more, she searched her pocket for a handkerchief but only found the sprig of pine tied with the faded pink ribbon. That was strange, she didn't remember taking it with her that morning.

The man moved again, and this time the smells of dung and dog hair were so strong Rose heaved. She was going to be sick.

'The window,' she gasped, 'please open the window. Quick.'

'I am sorry but I can't,' the man replied, gesturing to a lock at the top of the window. 'They're locked.'

4

In desperation, she buried her face into the sprig of pine, and took deep, long, calming breaths, hoping that the fresh scent of pine would stave off her nausea. Doctor Kilroy had been right about travelling in a post-coach. It was a nightmare.

When she was sure she wasn't going to be sick, she put the sprig of pine back inside her pocket and looked outside. It was pitch black with only a half moon watching over like a large yellow eye.

'Where are we?'

'We just passed Tongue.'

'Are we still on Lord McGunn's land?'

He shook his head. 'No, my lady, we're on McRae land.'

She closed her eyes to hide her relief. She was safe. Lord McGunn wouldn't come chasing after her now.

'I fear we'll have more snow before the morning,' the man carried on. 'I can feel it in my creakin' old bones. Lucky for me, I'm not too far from home now.'

He went on to explain that he would get off the coach the following morning at Borgie, talked about his business, his wife and bevy of children whilst Rose nodded politely.

The horn rang again. The horse's hooves rumbled on a cobbled courtyard and the coach shuddered and rattled to a halt.

'Lady and gentleman, time for a hot meal and a well-earned rest,' the post-guard announced with flourish as he opened the door.

He held out his hand to help Rose get down, taking hold of her elbow and giving it a little squeeze. Rose shivered as she walked across the courtyard towards the two-storey stone building. Lights glowed behind the steamed-up windows, giving it a warm, welcoming appearance. It would be so nice to sit by the fire and enjoy a hot meal, then sleep in a warm, comfortable bed…

She stopped in her tracks and turned to the post-guard.

'I can't go in.'

'Why is that, my lady?' He leant towards her, a puzzled look in his small, beady eyes.

'I have no money. Unless I can pay for food and lodgings with another necklace? What do you think?'

5

He flicked his hand in a dismissive gesture. 'Don't you worry about that. I'll settle the cost of your lodgings for you. We'll sort everything out later.'

'Thank you, you're very kind,' she told him with a sigh of relief. At least she wouldn't have to spend the night in the coach in the inn's stables.

He patted her arm and leaned closer.

'That's no problem. I couldn't leave a lovely young lady out in the cold, could I?' For a second, his eyes glittered with something other than bonhomie – something sinister and threatening – then it was gone and he smiled again.

Less than an hour later, Rose was getting undressed in her small bedroom on the first floor. She had gulped down a bowl of hot stew and two fat slices of bread before retiring for the night, leaving her travelling companions to their pints of ale, tumblers of whisky and game of cards.

The raucous noise of men's laughter and conversations from below drifted up through the floorboards. Shivering again, she hastily washed her face and hands in a bowl of lukewarm water before unpinning her hair, removing her boots and dress and slipping her nightdress on over her chemise.

The shawl she wrapped tightly around her shoulders didn't ward off the chill, so she spread her cloak over the blankets, and thought longingly about Lord McGunn's thick plaid and socks. If only she had them with her now, she wouldn't be so cold.

She held her breath, and her chest tightened.

McGunn.

By now he must know she had escaped.

She pictured his face as clearly as if he was there in front of her. His grey eyes, dark and stormy, his mouth unsmiling and the thick, dark stubble on his cheeks and long black hair which made him look like some warrior from a violent past. Never had a man deserved his nickname more than Lord McGunn, and even though she'd never seen him fight, she sensed that his nickname of 'claymore devil' suited him like a glove.

Her body tensed and she threw a nervous glance towards the door. She slid further into the bed, curled into a ball and pulled the covers over her head.

This was silly. Of course, McGunn wasn't about to barge into her room! She was well out of his reach, and in another day and a half, two at most, she would be reunited with Cameron and take her place by his side at Westmore.

The thought filled her with such sudden, overwhelming panic her mouth went dry and her heart raced frantically. Would Cameron still be angry with her or had he forgiven her? Would she find the frosty-eyed stranger who had boarded the *Sea Lady*, his face pale, his mouth twisted in a cruel scowl, or the handsome and witty man who had courted her?

She turned in the bed again and memories of their three wonderful weeks in Algiers flooded her mind.

Together they'd strolled the shaded lanes of the Jardin d'Essai – Algiers' enchanting new public garden overlooking the bay. They'd explored the Kasbah's narrow lanes, bought slices of juicy watermelon and melt-in-the-mouth honey and almond pastries from street stalls, and taken barouche rides in the hills outside Algiers or along the coast.

Cameron had been an attentive, devoted suitor with exquisite manners and dazzling charm. No man before him had brought her fresh bouquets, written poems which compared her eyes to a starry night. Akhtar urged caution and said it was a mistake to wed someone after such a short length of time. But he was an old man. What did he remember about being young and in love?

As for Malika … Rose swallowed hard as tears stung her eyes. Malika had disliked Cameron intensely, even going as far as inventing shocking lies about him. Cameron said Malika was jealous and, as much as it pained her to admit it, Rose thought he was probably right.

It didn't matter anymore. Malika was dead, buried in the little graveyard at Balnakeil. She would never smile, dance, or climb up orange trees with her again to get to the juiciest fruit. What had happened to her friend after they last argued, and who had killed her?

She clasped her fingers tightly together and listened to the sounds of laughter and talking until late during the night.

7

'Why are these people screaming and shouting?'

Rose pressed her nose against the window. The coach slowed to a walking pace as they entered a small village.

'And look at these poor children standing barefoot in the snow!'

Her travelling companion cleared his throat.

'It looks like the hamlet is being cleared.'

A cold fist tightened around Rose's heart.

'Cleared? You mean to say that odious man, Arthur Morven, is here?'

Her travelling companion nodded.

'I think that's him over there,' he said, pointing to a thick-set man wrapped in a dark grey cloak who sat on a black horse, away from the crowd.

As the coach reached the centre of the village, the noises of men shouting, women and children wailing and dogs barking became deafening. At the centre of it all, a dozen men ran around, holding torches or clubs and shoving people out of the way as they kicked down the doors of cottages, beating the animals and cattle with sticks and setting fire to houses.

On the side of the road, a little boy sat alone in the snow in blood-spattered clothes. He looked straight at Rose through huge, tear-filled eyes as the coach drove past, held his hand out and called, '*Màthair, Màthair!*'

'What is he saying?' Rose asked.

'I believe he wants his mother. She must be around here somewhere, gathering what's left of her things.'

With a cry of outrage, Rose pulled down the door handle and flung the door open. Enough was enough!

'What are you doing, are you mad?' The man next to her shouted.

'I'm going to talk to Morven, and make him stop this once and for all!'

She leapt forward, missed her step and landed on her knees but the snow cushioned her fall. Jumping to her feet, she pushed past a gang of young men who cheered as yet another house collapsed in a burning pile. Thugs, that's what they were, and

8

from the smell of whisky lingering around them, they were drunk too.

'Help me. Please, someone help me! My grandma's still in there.'

A woman beat her fists against the closed door of a nearby cottage. Plumes of smoke escaped from under the door, through the gaps in the shutters.

The woman ran to Morven who sat impassive on his horse, and clutched at his booted leg.

'Please, sir, I beg ye. Help me get her out, she's eighty-five and bed-ridden.'

He shook his leg so hard he kicked the woman in the chest and she stumbled backward with a cry of pain.

'Then the old crone's lived long enough and I'm doing you, and her, a favour.' He coughed and spat into the snow next to the woman.

So this was how her husband's factor replied to pleas for mercy. He was a monster, a criminal.

Rose squared her shoulders and marched up to him. Quivering with indignation, her breath short, she looked up into the man's ruddy face and met his blood-shot blue eyes.

'I order you to help this poor woman, right now.'

'And who might you be, my darling?' Morven's gaze travelled slowly, leisurely, from Rose's face down to her boots, then up again, in a way which made her blood boil and her face grow hot.

'I am Lady Rose McRae, and I order you to…'

'Lady Rose McRae, hey?' he cut in. 'I'm sorry, darling but the only Lady McRae I know is Lady Patricia.'

Rose let out a frustrated sigh. No one here would know about her, since Cameron was keeping their wedding a secret until the ball.

'Anyhow,' the big man resumed, 'I'm only obeying my lord's orders. He wants me to clear the strath of all these damned tenants before the end of the week and that's exactly what I'm doing.'

Did he dare claim that Cameron had ordered this? Rose swallowed hard and pointed to the flames which now licked the walls and roof of the house.

'But you can't leave an old woman trapped inside this house. She's going to die!'

Morven leant sideways towards her and she caught a whiff of his tobacco-smelling breath. 'That'll be one less mouth to feed; one less pauper on my lord's register.'

Rose stepped back with a cry of rage.

'You and your men are no better than murderers. Rest assured that I'll tell my husband all about this. Your days as Factor are numbered.'

If she had hoped to shock him, she was disappointed. He stared at her for a while then his fleshy lips twisted into a thin, cruel smile.

'We'll see, my darling, we'll see. For now my work here is done and I bid you a good day. Oh and by the way, I'll tell my Lord and Lady you're on your way when I next see them.'

He bowed his head in a mock salute, gave his horse a sharp heel kick and rode towards the mail coach. Rose saw him gesture to the guard who jumped down from his seat to talk to him. The men spoke for a couple of minutes then Morven rode away. His gang of men dispersed too, taking to their horses and starting in a rowdy convoy out of the burning village.

Rose looked at the pieces of wood, some half-burnt, charred and smouldering, that lay on the snowy ground. Grabbing hold of a thick, sturdy looking stick, she ran to the burning house the woman was still trying to get into.

'Get a stick and help me! We'll break the door down,' she instructed, before ramming the club into the door as hard as she could. It took the two of them and several attempts before the door cracked open and fell back.

'Grandma? Where are ye?' The woman shouted as she took a few steps inside.

Rose followed her cautiously, lifting her skirt right up to shield her face from the intense heat and thick black smoke. There was a loud whoosh sound when the roof caught fire and cinders started raining inside the cottage and onto her hair.

'I can see her. She's over there.' The woman darted forward, oblivious to the fire roaring around her.

There was nothing Rose could do. It took only a few seconds for the ceiling to collapse, engulfing the cottage, the woman and her grandmother into flames. She ran out and slipped to the ground, tears streaming from her burning eyes, and coughing so hard she could hardly catch her breath.

She didn't have the strength to protest when the post-guard lifted her in his arms and carried her away from the burning heap of rubble.

'What did you think you were doing? Are you crazy?' he shouted. 'You could have been killed.'

Her ears still filled with the thunderous roar of the fire, she hardly heard him. He put her down on the snowy ground and she raised her head to look at the fat, grey clouds in the sky above, saw white flakes swirl as they fell slowly to the ground. Sick and gripped with panic, she closed her eyes and shuddered uncontrollably.

These were ashes from the ruined village – from the houses, the people and animals Morven had set fire to – falling on the ground and all over her. Choking her.

Only when she felt wetness and cold slipping against her cheeks and into her neck did she realise it wasn't ash falling, but snow.

'We have to go, my lady,' the guard said, 'or we'll be late in Borgie.'

Numb, exhausted, she nodded and followed him to the coach. Before she climbed on board, she turned to survey the devastation her husband's men had left behind, the looks of desperation on people's faces as they searched the smoking ruins of their homes for whatever they could salvage.

'Where will these people go now?'

The post-guard shrugged.

'They'll find somewhere, a village on the coast, or Inverness, Dundee or Glasgow. But I gather most of them will make their way to Wrath. Lord McGunn won't turn them out. He never does.'

And he slammed the door shut.

11

Chapter Two

'So you're going after her?'

MacBoyd watched Bruce saddle Shadow from the stable doorway. Behind him the sky lit up with the first signs of daybreak – pale grey hues with a line of fire along the horizon.

'I have no choice. I need her to add weight to my *negotiations* with McRae,' Bruce growled. 'I must get her back here before she reaches Westmore and ruin my plans… or before she trips over a rock and falls down a cliff, or gets lost on the moors. The woman is a walking disaster.'

He paused and smiled. 'Then again the other passengers might throw her out of the mail coach when they tire of her calling them monkey names or silly McNames.'

MacBoyd's eyes widened. 'Monkey names? McNames? What on earth are you talking about?'

Bruce carried on buckling the saddle straps.

'When she doesn't say I'm a baboon or a macaque,' he explained. 'She calls me McGlum… or was it McGrouch?'

MacBoyd let out a booming laugh and slapped his big hands on his thighs.

'Either suits you, my friend, especially today. You've done nothing but rant and shout since you found out the lass didn't come back to the Lodge but sneaked out of the doctor's house and boarded the mail coach all on her own and without anyone paying any attention.' He shook his head. 'You must admit she outwitted you.'

Bruce clenched his jaw.

'She didn't outwit me at all,' he snarled. 'But she's resourceful, I'll grant you that.'

He glanced up at his friend. 'Stop grinning, it's not funny.'

'Lord McGunn?' Agnes called from the courtyard.

MacBoyd moved aside to let her pass. Bruce arched his eyebrows. His friend's cheeks looked very flushed suddenly, and he wondered if there was some kind of attachment between him and the young maid. She looked pretty flustered too…

'I packed some warm clothing and some food, like you asked.' Agnes gave MacBoyd a timid smile as she brushed past him and handed Bruce two leather bags and a flask.

'I also filled your flask with the whisky from your study; I thought you might need it.'

Bruce thanked her and slipped the flask into one of the bags. Agnes shifted on her feet, hesitant.

'Is there anything else?'

She blushed more deeply.

'I put Lady Rose's shoes in your bag too – the pretty ones she lost in the village that you asked me to retrieve for her. I think she'd be glad to have them back.'

'You asked Agnes to retrieve Rose's slippers?' MacBoyd arched his eyebrows.

'I wonder why I bothered. These silly shoes won't be any good in the snow,' Bruce muttered, aware of his friend's amused gaze. 'Anyway, it's time I left. I should catch up with the post-coach later today. It can't travel fast with this weather. I'll take the ferry boat across Loch Eriboll then another across Tongue Bay, and after that I'll ride flat out across the moors.'

MacBoyd pointed to the pistol at his side. 'I see you're expecting trouble.'

Bruce shrugged. 'There's no harm in being prepared, especially with Morven and his thugs roaming the roads these days.'

He slung a bag across his chest, led Shadow out into the courtyard.

'Take care of things in my absence,' he said as he swung onto the horse. 'It might be a couple of days, maybe more, before we come back.'

'Don't worry.' MacBoyd looked up at the sky and frowned. 'Get yourself and the woman back here safely. Another storm's on the way.'

14

'Aye, and we'll be right in the thick of it if I don't hurry,' Bruce agreed wearily. He bade his friend goodbye and rode out of the courtyard and onto the coastal path.

The coach had probably stopped at Tongue for the night. Its progress today would be hampered by the snow. If he rode hard and took short cuts, he'd catch up with it before the night – and the storm.

He rode like the devil, stopping only to take the ferry, rest the horse and have a bite to eat. As he travelled eastward the sky became heavier, lower, filled with threatening, lead-coloured and snow-laden clouds, but the storm held off.

It was late in the afternoon when he reached Borgie. Sheltering in a wooded valley on the banks of a fast flowing river, the village was on the main road to Melvich and the mail coach always stopped there.

'They're only a couple of hours ahead of you,' the landlady at the coaching inn said as she poured him a mug of strong, steaming hot tea.

'One of the horses had to be re-shod at the blacksmith. It was just as well they had a long break, if you ask me. Their poor lady passenger was very poorly.'

Bruce put his mug down on the counter and frowned.

'What was wrong with her?'

'She was in shock, poor lamb, crying and shaking like a leaf no matter how much hot tea and scones I fed her. I believe she saw Morven and his gang evict crofters this morning.' She looked at him, her face grim. 'I heard they burned the hamlet and two women died.'

Well, well...so Rose had seen for herself how McRae treated his tenants. She must have been so ashamed of him and his callous methods she hadn't even told the landlady who she really was.

The landlady finished wiping the counter with a damp cloth and looked up.

She gave him an appraising glance. 'Is she a friend of yours?'

He nodded and replied without thinking.

'She's a lot more than a friend.'

Rose was his security for the future of his estate against McRae's dishonest, underhand practices.

The landlady's eyes gleamed, she smiled and a sigh shook her generous bosom.

'Then she is a lucky lady.'

Damn. The woman had misunderstood him.

'No, it's not what you think. I mean, she is…'

The woman put her hand on his forearm and leant over the counter.

'You don't have to explain, Lord McGunn. She is very pretty, and very sweet.'

He opened his mouth to set her straight then sighed and shook his head. It didn't matter after all, let the woman believe what she wanted.

Light was fading when he left the inn. Looking up at the greyish-blue sky, he gathered he had about an hour of daylight left, which should be enough to catch up with the coach. He would get Rose out, and return with her to spend the night at the inn in Borgie. They would make their way back to Wrath in the morning – whether she wanted to or not.

Now, where had that bonnet gone?

Rose looked around the carriage, on the floor and between the seat and the side panel. Her blue bonnet was nowhere to be seen. She should never have taken it off to have that nap after leaving Borgie…

'Please my lady, hurry,' the coach driver called again from his box seat outside.

She glanced towards the window and frowned. She opened the carriage and stepped down.

'Where are we?'

She looked in dismay at the cluster of cottages and derelict outbuildings that huddled together in a forest clearing.

'Surely we're not stopping here for the night. The place looks abandoned.'

The post-guard averted his eyes and fumbled with the fastenings of his coat without answering. Rose examined her surroundings once again. No smoke came out of the chimneys.

No light glowed behind the grimy, broken glass or the wooden shutters covering the windows. No sound broke the thick silence of the forest except for the harsh crowing of ravens from the tree tops.

'Don't you worry, my lady, I know the people who live here. They'll look after you.'

People? What people? Before she could object once again, the post-guard grabbed hold of her bag and started towards a small cottage on the outskirts of the hamlet.

Rose turned to the coach driver who hadn't moved from his seat.

'Can we not return to the inn at Borgie? I don't like it here.'

The man shrugged but didn't look at her. 'It's too far.'

The mail guard stopped and turned round.

'Are you coming?' He too sounded impatient.

Puzzled, she followed him to a thatched cottage with shuttered windows. He lifted the bar off the hooks and opened the door then stepped aside.

'This way.'

She looked at him. 'Aren't you coming in too?'

'I forgot something in the coach. Make yourself comfortable, I won't be long.'

He handed her the bag and Rose took a tentative step inside. The cottage was dark inside, and even colder than outside. She breathed in dust and mould and sneezed.

'Wait a minute. No one lives here. You said there were peop...'

She didn't have time to finish. The post-guard gave her a hard shove in the back and slammed the door behind her. She heard the scrapping of a piece of wood being slotted into position to bar the door. By the time she realised she was being locked inside the old cottage, it was too late.

'Hey! What are you doing? Come back!'

It didn't make sense. Why would the guard abandon her?

She stuck her ear to the door and held her breath. Was this the sound of the coach rattling away on the path as it left the village? She pounded her fists on the door and gave frantic kicks, screamed for the men to come back.

No one answered. Silence and darkness soon fell, smothering like a thick blanket.

She turned away from the door, crossed her arms on her chest to stop herself from shaking and forced a few deep breaths down, but shivers of panic crawled all over her skin like spiders. This was her worst nightmare. She was trapped in total darkness, with not even the slightest glimmer of light filtering through the shutters. Her heart hammered hard against her ribs.

Perhaps she could make a fire...

She took a few cautious steps, her arms stretched out to feel for objects in the way. Her foot kicked a tin pot. The noise echoed like the ringing of a bell in the empty house. Biting her lip, she carried on and this time rammed her hip hard into the corner of a table.

'Bedbugs and stinky camels!'

Shouting wouldn't help. And neither would crying, she thought, as she wiped her eyes with the back of her hands. She had to keep her wits about her, make a fire, and get some light.

After fumbling in the dark for what felt like an eternity, she found the fireplace and knelt down on the cold, uneven stone floor. Her fingers touched a metal grate, burnt twigs and a pile of cold ashes. Whoever had made the last fire had long gone...

Frantic now, she rose to her feet and groped around for a piece of candle, a box of matches, a lamp. Please let there be something that she could use to light a fire!

There was nothing. As her eyes got used to the darkness, she could make out the shapes of furniture: a table and chairs, a dresser, and a bench along one of the walls, or perhaps it was a bed...

What had happened to the people living here? Where had they gone? A chilling thought went through her mind. What if they hadn't left but died and their decayed bodies still lay there? She could brush past them in the dark and wouldn't even know it.

No! Don't think about that. Think about nice things. Think about riding out on the plains in the sunshine, about the flowers in the garden. Think about Bou Saada...

Bou Saada. Home. Thousands of miles away from here.

She sat down on the flagstone next to the fireplace and wrapped her arms around her knees. It was so cold she couldn't stop shivering. It was so dark she could hardly breathe. Yet somehow she would have to survive the night, the cold, and the fear of the darkness.

Where the hell were they? He should have met the coach by now. He'd ridden as far as Melvich where no one had seen the coach yet. He had then gone back on himself, asking travellers along the way. Every time the answer was the same. No one had seen the post-coach, it was as if it had disappeared from the surface of the earth.

He came to a stone cross marking a crossroads and reined Shadow in. The horse neighed softly. Its breath steamed in the cold night. Bruce narrowed his eyes to survey his surroundings. Damn, it was cold. He pulled his flask out of the bag, unscrewed the top and drank a sip of whisky.

A feeling of dread weighed down on his chest. Something was wrong. Even if the coach was stranded with a broken wheel or an injured horse, he would have come upon it by now. No, something else had happened.

Shadow stumbled over a rock. Bruce patted its neck, issued a few reassuring words. The horse was exhausted and he ran the risk of causing it a serious injury if he rode any longer. He would spend the night at Leckfurin or Bettyhill and resume his search at first light. He drank a little more whisky, wiped his mouth with the back of his hand and put the flask back in the bag.

Then he heard it – the unmistakable rattling of a horse-drawn carriage driving at speed on the road. It was them, at last.

He jumped to the ground and stood in the middle of the road. The coach driver and the post-guard might need a little persuading to relinquish their passenger. Willing or not, Rose McRae would come back with him, and he wouldn't let anybody stand in his way.

It wasn't long before the mail coach appeared on the track.

'Hey you! Move off that road.' The driver bellowed as he reined the horses in and the coach slowed down to a walking pace, then came to a creaking halt.

'I said move off.' He waved his whip and the lash whistled as it sliced through the air.

'I want to speak to your lady passenger,' Bruce shouted back.

'What passenger? We have no passenger.' The driver shook his head. 'Stand aside at once. It's a criminal offence to delay the mail coach.'

Bruce stood his ground. 'You have a lady passenger and I mean to speak to her. I'm Lord McGunn, damn it. Do you not recognise me?'

The driver nodded, shifted on his seat. 'Aye, but...'

'Then you should know better than to argue with me.' He started towardss the side of the coach.

'What's going on, Angus?' A voice called from the back. The post-guard, no doubt.

'Lord McGunn says he wants to speak to the lady,' the driver replied in a slightly shaky voice.

'Tell him there's no lady on board,' the voice shouted back.

'There you are,' the driver spoke again. 'I told you. It's just the guard and me tonight.'

'You don't mind if I take a look, do you?'

Without waiting for an answer Bruce stepped forward and swung the door open. Rose was on board. She had to be.

The coach was empty, but there on the floor, stuck between the seat and the carriage's side panel, was a blue bonnet – the very same she'd worn at the church service the day before. He picked it up, shoved it in his coat pocket and jumped down.

'Where is she? What have you done with her?'

'I don't know who you're talking about.' The driver's voice shook even more.

'You know exactly who I'm talking about,' Bruce growled as he climbed onto the first step and reached out to grab the man's collar.

'You really don't want to make me angry.' Bruce pulled him close. 'This is the last time I'm asking you. Where the hell is she?'

The driver opened his mouth a few times but no sound came out.

'There's no need to shout, Lord McGunn.' The post-guard walked up to him.

Bruce let go of the driver's collar and turned to face him.

'The young lady wasn't feeling well so we left her at the inn in Bettyhill,' the man said. 'The landlord there promised to look after her.'

Bruce frowned. It was possible, of course, but he couldn't help feeling the man was lying.

'Then we'll go back to Bettyhill together,' he said, calling their bluff.

The driver let out a loud gasp. 'If we do that, we'll be late arriving in Melvich and…'

'You're late anyway. A couple of hours won't make much difference now. Lead the way and I'll follow.'

He turned his back to the post-guard and started walking towards Shadow, his hand resting lightly on the butt of his pistol as he braced himself for the attack.

Sure enough, he heard the rapid footfall behind him. One, two, three…fool!

He twisted sideways, lifted his arm up and struck the post-guard with a single blow to the face. The man fell backward, unconscious.

'I wouldn't if I were you.'

Bruce pulled his pistol out of the holster in a fluid move and aimed at the coach driver who was trying to pull a rifle out of his box seat.

With a curse, he lifted his hands up in the air.

'It wasn't my idea, I swear, Lord McGunn. Everything's his fault!' He pointed at the post-guard lying on the ground. 'He said we'd share the reward.'

So the two rascals wanted to trade Rose for a ransom. Bruce armed his pistol.

'What did you do with her?'

At his feet, the post-guard moaned and tried to move but Bruce stuck his boot across his throat and pressed down hard until the man let out a hard cough and stopped moving.

He narrowed his eyes and focused once more on the driver. His vision suddenly blurred and he blinked a few times.

'We left her in a cottage in an abandoned hamlet south of Borgie,' the driver answered.

'Where exactly?' Bruce raised an impatient hand to his forehead and wiped beads of perspiration.

Damn, the headache had come back with a vengeance. He was having another attack. His throat was dry, his heart pounded, his head felt like it was squeezed in a vice.

'I asked you where she was.' His voice now sounded weak and hoarse.

'*Sith Coille.*'

Bruce nodded. Fairy Wood. He knew where that was. His hand started shaking so badly he had to concentrate hard to keep the pistol aimed at the driver.

'Who's with her?'

The coach driver shook his head.

'Nobody. The hamlet is empty. It was cleared last summer. We thought she'd be fine there on her own for a day or two.'

Bruce took a few deep breaths and wiped his forehead with his sleeve this time.

'You mentioned a reward,' he said.

'Aye. It was Morven who told us to keep hold of the young lady. He said she was a troublemaker and that his Lord McRae would be very grateful and pay us handsomely if we held her up and stopped her from reaching Westmore.'

Nothing the man said made any sense. Why would Morven want to stop Rose from being reunited with her husband? Never mind that, he'd think about it later.

'Get some rope from your box seat and get down here.' He'd tie both men up, shove them inside then drive the coach to *Sith Coille* to get Rose, with Shadow tied at the back.

The man nodded. 'Yes, sir, straightaway, but you must believe me. I didn't want to do it, I swear, he made me…'

'Shut up and do as I say.'

22

Just then he swayed and dropped the pistol as a terrible pain gripped his chest. Hell, it hurt even to breathe, and his head now felt about to explode. He dropped to his knees, his pistol fell from his hand and he fell forward. The guard threw him a surprised glance and scrambled to his feet.

'What's wrong with him? He looks ill.' The driver called to the guard.

'I don't know and I don't care,' the guard mumbled. 'Let me finish him off then we can get out here. Blast, I can't find his pistol. Throw me your rifle.'

Bruce knew he had to do something or the guard would shoot him there and then. He felt the ground for his weapon. It had fallen close by, he was sure of it, yet his fingers only grasped small rocks, dirt from the road and frozen tufts of grass.

He hissed a sharp breath. Where was that damned pistol? He reached out a little further, and his fingers found the weapon at last. It took all his strength to flip his body over and sit up, then to lift his arm and shoot.

The shot went wide but sent the horses into a panic.

'Let's go,' the driver yelled over the racket of the horses neighing and stomping on the ground. 'Forget about him, he looks half dead anyway!'

With a shaky hand, Bruce re-armed the pistol and shot again. This time the bullet sent sparks into the night as it pinged against the side of the coach. Unable to stay upright any longer, he collapsed and his head hit the frozen ground.

He heard the hiss of the driver's whip, followed by the thunder of hooves and the creaking of the wheels as the coach started on the road towards him, and barely had time to scramble out of its way before it shot past, sending grit flying into his face.

Chapter Three

It was early evening in Bou Saada.

Dusk's lengthening shadows stretched across the garden. Touched by the last rays of sunshine, sandy Saharan plains shone like gold and distant mountain peaks hovered, a mauve haze above the line of the horizon. A light breeze whispered through the palm. It rustled the leaves of jujube, pomegranate and orange trees and carried the rhythmic, woody singing of cicada. The air was thick with fragrances – sweet, sensual, earthy fragrances of rose and jasmine, mint, sage and thyme, but the most potent of all was the scent of the oasis beyond the garden walls. Lush, moist, intoxicating.

A man's voice called her name and Rose's lips stretched into a smile. Hope surged inside her. Her prayers had been answered. Her father was home, at last. She ran so fast she felt she was flying. Her babouches crunched the multicoloured gravel on the garden lane. She grazed her arm on a cactus as she brushed past it but hardly felt the sting on her skin.

Her father sat on the low wall overlooking the town, a small, leather-bound book stamped with the imperial eagle in his hand. His military journal. He turned to her. He hadn't changed at all. His eyes were the same piercing blue, his hair just as dark and his face as weathered as she remembered. He put the book down, smiled and opened his arms wide. She nestled against his chest, laughing and crying at the same time as he ruffled her hair.

'You came back,' was all she could say.

'Listen, darling Rose,' he said. 'I don't have time to explain.'

'Explain what?'

'The medal. You must find the medal.'

'What medal?'

A roll of thunder resounded above them, so loud it drowned her father's voice. The sky darkened at once, shadows engulfed the garden and an icy wind swept across the oasis, creeping inside her body and chilling her to the bones. Her father spoke again and pointed to the diary, but she still couldn't hear him. Then he too started to fade into the shadows.

He was leaving her, again.

'Father,' she called. 'Don't leave me again.'

The thunder got louder. Her father had already left.

She opened her eyes and glanced around. There was no garden, no Bou Saada and no golden Sahara sands in the distance. In their place was only darkness and fear. She remembered where she was – an empty old house, in the middle of the forest. She had fallen asleep sitting next to the hearth, huddled in her cloak to keep warm. It was the thunder that had woken her.

She held her breath and listened.

This was no thunder, but the rumbling of a galloping horse. Someone was coming this way. She jumped to her feet and rushed to the door, bumping into a chair and the table on the way.

'Help! Help me please. I can't get out.'

She called out, again and again until she heard footsteps outside. The door rattled as the bar was dislodged then thrown onto the ground with a thumping noise. The handle shook but the door didn't open.

'Move back. The door's locked. I'm going to kick it in,' a man's deep voice said.

Her heart skipped a beat. Her mouth became dry.

'Lord McGunn? By Old Ibrahim's Beard, is that really you?'

He didn't answer but repeated his instruction, and this time she took a few steps back. A resounding crash echoed in the empty house and the door smashed open against the wall.

Lord McGunn stood still, his tall figure filling the door frame, darker than the night itself.

'Are you all right? They didn't...hurt you, did they?'

26

She could hardly see his face or the expression in his eyes but from the gruff, weary tone of voice, she knew he was annoyed.

She shook her head. 'No, the post-guard locked me in here then left. I don't understand why.'

'You're married to one of the richest men in Scotland, that's reason enough.'

She frowned. 'You mean to say that they wanted to trade me for a ransom?'

'Aye.'

She bit her lip. 'Where are they now?'

'My guess is that they're trying to put as much distance as they can between themselves and me.' He added, his voice mean and hard. 'But I'll get to them soon enough, don't you worry about it.'

'How did you find me?'

'I ran into the coach on the road to Melvich.'

'That was…ahem…lucky.' Or not; she hadn't made her mind up yet.

He stared at her. 'Luck had nothing to do with it. I've been chasing after you since dawn.'

He glanced towards the broken door. 'Listen, it's snowing. I need to find shelter for my horse. We're staying here tonight.'

Reluctant to step back alone into the dark room, Rose stood in the doorway despite the cold wind blowing snowflakes all over her, and watched as he kicked open a barn door and pulled Shadow inside. By the time he came back, two bags hung over his shoulders, her teeth clattered with cold. Without a word, he fumbled inside one of the bags, pulled out a candle and a box of matches and at long last there was light. He handed the candle to Rose, slotted the door back into place and slammed it shut.

Rose lifted the candle in front of her to take a good look at the small room. There were no decomposing bodies, no skeletons or rats scurrying along the walls, just a table and chairs, a dresser and a couple of shelves on the walls and a bed tucked away in a corner.

Lord McGunn found a broken dish on the dresser and asked her for the candle back. He poured a few drops of melted wax onto the plate, stuck the candle in the middle and frowned as he turned to her.

'You don't look well.'

His words bit into her self-esteem.

'I could say the same about you,' she retorted.

With dark stubble covering his cheeks and the tips of his raven-black hair touching his shoulders, he looked more than ever like a warrior from an ancient and untamed past. Tonight, however, he was also pale, with deep lines framing his mouth and dark shadows under his eyes.

Her chest tightened. It was probably her fault he was tired. He had ridden all day to catch up with the coach and rescue her.

'I suppose I must thank you for coming after me,' she started, hesitant.

'Don't bother,' came his sharp reply. 'I only hope you learnt your lesson. Your silly escapade could have ended in tragedy. You could have frozen to death, here on your own. Or worse.'

So much for gratitude! A sudden flash of anger heated her face and made her pulse race. Without thinking she stepped forward and jabbed her finger into his chest.

'Did you really expect me to go along with what you were planning to do?'

He caught her wrist in a steely grip and bent down towards her slowly, until she felt his breath on her face and saw the dark specks of slate in his eyes.

'You mean, what I am *still* planning to do,' he said in a cold, calm voice. 'As soon as the weather lifts, I'll take you back to Wrath then ride to Westmore. I won't let your husband ruin me or my estate. If he wants you and his clipper back, he'll have to agree to my terms.'

She gasped and tears filled her eyes.

'So my running away was all for nothing…'

'It was indeed. And don't even think of trying that again because I will always find you.'

He pulled her a little closer, and she felt the heat of his body against her.

'Wherever you go, wherever you hide, I will find you and drag you back to Wrath with me,' he repeated, enunciating every syllable before releasing her.

'For now, I'll make a fire and get us a drink and something to eat.'

He walked to the fireplace, knelt down next to a basket filled with kindling and logs and started building a fire. He struck a match, slipped it into the pile and soon flames rose and crackled, bathing the small room in a golden glow and throwing huge shadows on the walls.

He lifted one of the bags onto the table and proceeded to unpack some food – a loaf of oatmeal bread, a piece of cheese wrapped in thin cloth, a few wrinkled apples.

'That should last us a couple of days, until we can leave this place.'

'A couple of days?'

'I doubt the snowstorm be over sooner.'

Panic made her heart flutter.

'But what will Cameron think if he finds out I spent even one night alone with you?'

Surprisingly, a slow smile stretched his lips.

'It wouldn't be the first time, now would it, sweetheart?'

She blushed so fiercely even her ears felt like they were burning.

'I didn't spend the night with you! I was in your bed less than five minutes, ten at most, and you know it.'

She bit her lip and wished she could take the words back.

'I wasn't talking about that time,' he replied, 'but about the night of the Northern Lights.'

'The Northern Lights?' As soon as she spoke, elusive images of a dreamlike sky filled with colourful and shimmering patterns flickered in her memory.

'What about them?' she asked, but a feeling of unease crept inside her.

Ignoring her, McGunn picked up a large cooking pot and took two earthenware tumblers from a shelf.

'I'll get some water from the stream and wash those cups, so we can have a hot drink,' he declared before opening the door and going out into the night.

'Wait! Tell me…' She shouted after him, but he was already gone.

Restless, she paced the floor for what felt an eternity. What did he mean about them spending the night together? And what on earth was taking him so long?

At last he came back. He opened the door, letting a blast of cold wind and snowflakes into the cottage.

'What should I remember?' she asked as soon as he walked in.

He shook the snow off his boots, pushed the door shut with his shoulder and carried the cooking pot to the fireplace.

'That'll take a while to heat up,' he said as he hanged the pot to a hook above the fire Next he pulled the two tumblers out of his coat pockets and placed them on the table.

She stepped closer. 'I asked you a question.'

'And I heard you.' He unbuttoned his coat, shrugged it off then looked straight at her.

'What do you remember about the Northern Lights?'

'They were beautiful lights in the sky.'

'That's a start. What else?'

She frowned. 'Nothing… I hope you're not implying that I slept in your room that night.'

'Well, you weren't exactly in my room,' he said, throwing his wet coat on a chair.

'So I wasn't in your…ahem… bed?'

'No.'

She blew a sigh of relief. 'That's all right then.'

He said nothing as he sat at the table, pulled a knife out his pocket and proceeded to cut the bread into thick slices. When he'd finished, he looked up and said.

'Not really. You see, sweetheart… you were sitting very comfortably in my lap, in front of the fireplace.'

The blood drained from her face. She swayed against the table.

'What?'

'That's not all. I woke up at dawn and was about to take you back to your room when some of my staff came in and saw you.'

A terrible foreboding now crept into her heart. Her mouth, her throat became dry. She swallowed hard.

'People saw me? How many?'

'One or two.' He grimaced. 'Make it a dozen.'

Her legs were suddenly too weak to carry her. She pressed her hand against her heart and collapsed on the bench opposite him.

'This is awful,' she whispered at last. 'What must people think of me?'

This time he grinned.

'That you're just another woman who succumbed to my charm? I suppose it could be worse. At least you were dressed – in a fashion.'

'In a fashion?' she squeaked. 'What was I wearing?'

His grin widened. 'A very fetching combination of frilly nightshirt, thick woolly socks – mine, I reckon – and cute little boots.'

'This isn't funny!' She snapped. 'Why didn't you wake me up before the morning?'

'Believe me, sweetheart, I tried, but you're one hell of a deep sleeper.'

She closed her eyes. The Northern Lights – the Merry Dancers, wasn't that what he had called them that night? Fragments of memory now rushed back to her: disjointed images of Lord McGunn standing on the cliff edge under a magical, colourful night sky. He was cold, and drunk, and she had walked him back to his tower, helped him take off his shirt in front of the fire. She swallowed hard as more pictures of that night played back. He sat down in his armchair. Then she had a sip of that awful tonic and fainted. So it was true!

'It was that horrible liquor I drank that made me sick,' she said, her eyes still closed. 'I poured some out in a glass for you and drank a little, then everything became blurred and I fell into a great big black hole.'

'Into my lap, more like.'

She blushed again. Even in the dim light he could see the pink heat on her cheeks. He'd never met a woman who blushed so violently and so easily before. An image which had tormented him before flashed in his mind – that of creamy white throat and breasts taking on the same delicious shade of pink. He rose and walked to the fireplace. Grabbing a stick, he bent down and started poking at the fire. Sparks rose and flew up in ribbons into the chimney.

What was the matter with him? He usually had more self-control when women were concerned, yet he only had to remember how deliciously soft and curvy Rose had felt under him for red-hot desire to surge and thrust inside him, and make his body hard and achy.

'You drank some whisky?' he asked in a gruff voice.

'It wasn't whisky but medicinal tonic, and so disgusting it made me all weak and fuzzy.'

'That explains the broken glass.' He turned to her. 'Why did you go to the cliffs that night?'

'A… dream woke me, and then I saw the lights outside and I just wanted to be close to the sky.' She gave him a stern look. 'It was fortunate I did. You were so drunk you could have fallen off the cliff.'

He didn't answer but set his mouth in a grim line. He must have suffered another attack of his unpredictable, debilitating illness. Even if Kilroy was right and he did sleepwalk, there was definitely something else ailing him. Whatever it was, he could only hope he had time to secure the future of his estate before it killed him.

The water started bubbling in the pot. He filled up two tumblers, sprinkled tea leaves into the boiling water and handed her a cup. Wrinkling her nose, she picked out the brown leaves floating on the surface with her fingers while he cut the cheese and placed a wedge in front of her together with some bread and an apple.

Outside, the blizzard gathered pace as it swept through the forest and filled the night with howling and screeching, and the sounds of trees groaning like spectres. The wind rattled the door, clawed at the shuttered window, and Rose let out a startled cry when a strong gust hurled down the chimney and made the fire hiss and spit.

'There's no need to be afraid,' he said, calmly. 'We're perfectly safe here. These cottages were solidly built.'

She nodded but her face remained pinched, and her eyes huge and frightened. He bit into an apple, stretched his legs in front of him and crossed them at the ankles. The pains in his head and chest had receded at last, as had the feverish tremors, and a pleasant torpor now filled him. For the first time in days, he felt almost at peace.

'What will you do when the storm has passed?' Rose asked, breaking the silence.

'I told you. I'll take you back to Wrath then I'll ride to Westmore to talk to McRae about arrangements concerning you and the *Sea Eagle*… and about Malika, of course.'

'Take me with you.'

She leant forward, put her hand on his forearm.

'Please.'

Her lips parted and he caught a glimpse of her pearly white teeth and the tip of her tongue. He remembered exactly how her lips had felt under the pad of his thumb – soft, yielding and moist. His breathing deepened, his blood pumped around his body, hot and sluggish.

'Cameron must be told about Morven at once. The man must be stopped and thrown into jail.' Oblivious to the turmoil inside him, she pressed her fingers harder onto his arm. 'The sooner that despicable man is punished, the sooner we can give these poor people their houses back, or start building new ones.' Her lips quivered. 'I saw what he was capable of this morning. He stood aside while his gang burned houses down. Two women died because of him.'

Glancing down, she withdrew her hand from his arm.

He sighed, dragged his fingers through his hair but didn't say anything. It would be useless. Rose clearly still didn't believe Morven was only following McRae's orders.

'What's more, I want to be the one telling Cameron about Malika,' she added. 'Even though they didn't exactly get along, I know he'll be eager to start an enquiry.'

'I doubt he'll be that bothered by the death of a dancing girl,' he snorted.

She looked straight at him, her eyes shining like gems and her golden curls a halo of sunshine in the light of the fire.

'That proves you don't know him. He is a good man. I wouldn't have married him if he wasn't.'

'A good man?'

He felt angry suddenly, so angry he wanted to break something – McRae's neck preferably.

He forced a deep breath in. What did he care if Rose was wrong about McRae? A few weeks of married life would soon dispel her illusions. McRae couldn't live without his whoring, drinking and gambling clubs. Rose wasn't the first, and wouldn't be the last, to be fooled by his charming façade. The man was a debauched, wicked, thrill-seeking cad.

Then again, who was *he* to talk? He may not share McRae's predilection for prostitutes and card tables. He may not turn tenants away from their homes in the dead of winter, but his heart and soul were just as black. The nightmares which haunted him were stark reminders of his past actions, and his illness was no doubt the product of his tormented and feverish brain. Didn't his grandfather predict that he would end up mad like his mother, or drinking with the devil like his father – whoever *he* was?

He got up so abruptly the feet of the chair scraped the floor.

'Enough talking, it's time to rest. Drink up, finish your food and go to bed.'

He pulled his plaid out of his bag and handed it to her. 'Take this. It will keep you warm.'

He knelt in front of the hearth to add more wood onto the grate.

Her footsteps pattered on the floor, her skirt rustled softly behind him and brushed against his back. He breathed in her fragrance and closed his eyes. All he wanted to do right now was to hold her in his arms, brush her hair aside and bury his face in the curve of her neck to taste the softness of her skin and her unique, sunny and feminine scent.

He took hold of a thick stick and poked at the fire.

'I didn't think it was possible, but I swear you're even more bad-tempered than my brother, and that's not an easy feat,' she started in an angry voice. 'I will eat and drink when I please, and go to bed when I'm tired. I am sick of you ordering me about as if I were silly, naive and irresponsible. You may not have noticed, Lord McGunn. I am not a child but a grown woman.'

Hell, of course he had noticed. He stabbed at the fire with his stick. She was the woman who made him smile and dream of sunshine and summer days – the woman who aroused his most primitive instincts. She was also the woman he would never have because she was McRae's.

He tightened his grip on the stick, turned round and rose to his feet.

'But you are silly, naive and irresponsible,' he started, coldly. 'So let's be very clear, *sweetheart*. I don't care a jolt about your spoilt brat antics. You're not on your Algerian estate here, ordering your servants about and cracking your whip to scare them off. I'm in charge, which means you'll you do what the bloody hell I tell you to do. Understood?'

The stick snapped in his hand and he threw the pieces in the fire.

When he turned round again, he was surprised to see tears in her eyes.

'How dare you speak to me like this?' Her voice shook. 'It is true I misjudged the intentions of the post-guard and the coach driver,' she carried on in a choked voice. 'It is also true I'm not clever. I'm nothing like my mother or Harriet, my brother's wife. I can't read a serious book without falling asleep and if I don't concentrate really hard when I help Akhtar with the accounts I get all the figures mixed up...'

She was so pretty with her pink cheeks and her shiny blue eyes that he had trouble concentrating on what she was saying. Why was she saying she wasn't bright? Hell. The woman could speak French, English and Arabic, and if that wasn't clever, he didn't know what was.

'But I'm not a spoilt brat,' she resumed, 'and I don't crack the whip to anyone. We only have a few servants in Bou Saada and they're like family to us.'

Her words penetrated the thick mist of his consciousness. He shook his head.

'Hang on a minute… So what you said that first day about whipping your servants, it was a lie?'

She shrugged. 'Of course.'

'And you're not rich?'

She shook her head. 'Our estate was confiscated by the French army over a year ago and was only recently given back to us in a pitiful state. My brother offered to help us rebuild it, but my mother is a very proud woman. She would never accept charity from anyone, let alone her own son.'

'Does McRae know you're not rich?'

'Of course.'

'Then why did he marry you?'

Her blue eyes opened wider.

'He married me because he loves me.'

'Love?' he sneered. 'Marriage is a business arrangement, especially where McRae is concerned.'

Her cheeks turned a deep shade of red.

'You are truly the most horrid man I ever met. How I wish you'd fallen off that cliff the other night or that your Merry Dancers had come to take you away!'

She darted to the door, grabbed hold of the handle, managed to pull the door open onto the cold, stormy night, but he was right behind her. He slammed the door shut.

'Where do you think you're going?'

She spun round, her back against the door. He put his hands on either side of her head, caging her in.

'Outside. And I don't care if I freeze to death. Anywhere is better than being stuck here with you. You hated me from the very minute I arrived at Wrath Harbour. It's a wonder you bothered to come after me at all.'

Mesmerized by her mouth, so tantalisingly close, he bent down slowly. His heart beat fast, driven by a need so powerful he was losing control.

36

She was trapped between the hard, cold wooden door and his hard, hot body, and even though he wasn't touching her she was completely at his mercy. His gaze skimmed over her eyes, her face, down to her throat and her chest which rose with every fast, shallow breath she took. She was no match for him. It would be so easy to kiss her and take her, here and now.

He closed the gap between them until her breasts brushed against his chest and their hips made contact.

She gasped and fear made her eyes grow wide. It was like a slap in the face. What the hell was he doing, forcing himself onto a woman?

He pulled away, and stepped back inside the room.

'I already told you. I'm protecting my interests,' he said, bringing a note of harshness into his voice. 'As long as I have you, McRae will have to do what I say and call his bankers off.'

'So I'm just a pawn in your bitter war against my husband. That's the only reason you came after me?'

He nodded. 'Of course, what else?'

'Then you really are no better than the post-guard and his accomplice, are you?'

He flinched, his jaw locked. 'No, I suppose I'm not,' he conceded. His fists balled at his sides, he turned away.

'Please do as I say,' he finished. 'Go to bed now.'

Moving away from the door, Rose didn't argue this time but wrapped herself into the plaid and lay down on the filthy straw mattress.

Bruce sat down, pulled his flask and poured himself a drink. It was going to be a long night.

Chapter Four

Her eyes flicked open onto thick, velvety darkness. Outside the wind howled and swished, and for one terrifying moment she thought she was back on the *Sea Eagle* in the middle of the storm. Then she remembered. She wasn't on the clipper but in a cottage in the forest and a blizzard raged outside. Inside however, everything was still, silent and empty.

Her heart leapt with panic. She was alone in the dark. Again.

With Lord McGunn's plaid still tightly wrapped around her, she jumped off the bed and walked to the fireplace where a few embers still cast a weak glow from under a pile of ashes. She grabbed hold of a stick and poked at the embers until they gave out enough light for her to see that the candle's stump stood in a pool of congealed wax on the table, next to Lord McGunn's open flask and his pistol, but where was he?

She spotted the shape of a body stretched out on the floor behind the table and her eyes skimmed over a man's riding boots, black breeches, a white shirt.

'Lord McGunn, I don't think sleeping on the floor is a good idea,' she called.

He didn't move, make a sound or open his eyes. And he called her a deep sleeper!

'At least put your jacket or your coat on…'

He didn't even stir. Was he even breathing? By Old Ibrahim's Beard, what if he had drunk too much whisky and had passed out? Or even worse, what if he was dead and she was on her own in that abandoned shed in a middle of a snowstorm?

In a panic, she knelt down at his side, slipped her hand over his shirt to pat his chest. He wasn't dead. His heart was beating,

39

faint and erratic. Her hand slid up to his shoulder and she gave him a shake.

'Lord McGunn. Wake up.'

His breath caught in his throat and he moaned.

'Wake up!' She shook him harder.

He opened his eyes and grimaced in pain, his hand clasped his chest.

'Hell, it hurts,' he groaned.

'What's the matter with you?'

He heaved a few laboured, raspy breaths.

'I think it's over…this time.'

'What do you mean, it's over? You drank too much whisky again, didn't you? Don't even think of denying it. Your flask is over there, on the table. That's the second time I've seen it happen. You should know it doesn't agree with you.'

'Quiet. Stop chattering… and let me… let me die in peace.'

Panic squeezed her chest in a tight, cold fist.

'Nonsense! You're not going to die and leave me all alone here, do you hear?'

He blinked. 'Would be hard not to, with you shouting in my ear.'

At least he was talking, even if he sounded weak. That had to be a good sign.

She rose to her feet and looked around the room.

She needed more light, and to get the fire going again. She searched his bag, pulled a new candle out of the front pocket and lit it. Her throat tightened when she looked at him again. In the glow of the candle, his face was gaunt, his lips grey and his eyes dark, so dark they were almost hollow. He did look ill, more than ill. He looked haunted.

What if he really was going to die? Fear tightened her chest, panic made her heart flutter. She threw a handful of twigs and a couple of logs on the fire, struck a match. Flames rose, curled timidly around the logs at first, then jumped higher.

'Let's get you warm,' she said, hurrying to his side. 'Can you stand up?'

'Leave me. I told you… it's too late… this time,' he said in an exhausted whisper.

40

'No, I'll help you.'

She slipped her hands under his arms and pulled him up in a sitting position. He was so weak he sagged against her. Gritting her teeth, she slipped her hands under his arms again, pulled and pushed, panting with the effort. It took three attempts but he eventually managed to sit up.

She then grabbed hold of his boots, slid her hands slowly along his calves, along his strong, muscular thighs, and she tried to fold his legs up. His body shuddered under her touch. He opened his eyes and shot her a stare as hot as molten lead.

'What the hell are you doing?'

'Helping you…'

'I said to leave me alone.'

She curled her hands on her hips and smiled.

'I never thought I would say this, but I'm actually glad to hear your grumpy voice. If you have the strength to be cantankerous, then you can't be feeling that bad. Anyway, whether you want it or not, I'm not leaving you on this cold, dirty floor.'

She patted his knees and added an authoritative 'Don't move', before slipping her hands under his armpits again.

'Now, push with your heels into the floor while I lift you up.'

She heaved, pulled, pushed and panted until at last he was up on his feet. Then wrapping both arms around his waist to support him, she staggered with him towards the fireplace.

'Sit on that chair while I make some tea.'

He flinched as he collapsed into the chair, and lifted his hand to his chest again.

'Is your chest hurting?' she asked, kneeling down in front of him and gently brushing his hair back from his forehead.

Her anger melted away at once, and she was shaken by a potent blend of compassion, helplessness and the inexplicable urge to stroke his face, his hair, and make him well again.

He gave a weak nod. 'My head too. Always my head.'

'And you're sure it's not because you drank too much whisky?'

She cast a doubtful eye towards the flask and the tumbler on the table. She didn't care what he'd say, the thing was vile and she would dispose of it at the earliest opportunity.

He squeezed his eyes shut, took a few shallow breaths.

'It's not the whisky. I've had these fits before, but they're getting worse.'

He paused. 'I know what it is… It's the curse.'

'What curse?'

'My curse. Here.' He pointed to his chest and spoke in a strange language. '*Ahankar*.'

'You mean – the tattoo?' Her breath became short, her face warm, as she remembered the dark blue letters stencilled just above his heart. 'What does it mean?'

He closed his eyes and spoke barely unintelligible words.

'Pride. Mine. Ferozeshah. It's because of me it happened… It's my curse, my own bloody fault my men died.'

His voice broke and he slumped against the back of the chair.

He might be delirious but she had to keep him awake until he'd had a hot drink.

'What happened at Ferozeshah?' she asked, even if she already knew about it. Cameron had told her about McGunn's debacle in the Punjab. It was the reason he had been dismissed from the army.

'I didn't know you were… interested in war and… battles.' He spoke slowly, wincing with every word.

'Don't forget my father was a colonel in Napoleon's Cuirassiers. I grew up listening to his battle stories. He and my brother would discuss strategy and battle tactics. Actually, I think you might be interested in some of the accounts in his war diary…'

The words died on her lips as a vague memory fluttered into her consciousness then fluttered right out again. She held her breath, closed her eyes. It was something about the diary, something important. She shook her head. Now wasn't the time or the place to think about her father's diary. She had to concentrate on making Lord McGunn better.

'Please, tell me about Ferozeshah,' she insisted.

Bruce straightened up in the chair. Kicking the pain out of his mind, he breathed in, long and deep, and gathered his thoughts and memories. He never talked about it, hadn't mentioned it since the enquiry and his dismissal from the army.

'Are you sure you really want to know?'

Rose nodded.

'Very well. My plan was risky. I knew it, yet I pushed ahead without waiting for my colonel's go ahead.' He stopped to catch his breath.

'General Gough's earlier attack against the Sikh camp at Ferozeshah was rushed and poorly planned. The men were exhausted. Our eighteen-pounder guns were still at Mudki and we had no heavy artillery. By nightfall we had lost hundreds of men and gained no ground.'

He closed his eyes. Suddenly he was back in the hell of that day – the relentless push through the jungle to reach the Sikh lines, the fire of enemy artillery on the plains causing such dense smoke it was hard to breathe and see the way forward; then the ferocious hand-to-hand combat and horrific injuries inflicted to his men by the Sikh warriors' *Kirpan*.

'I decided to infiltrate the Sikh camp with my unit, neutralise them from the inside and blow up their ammunition depot. My unit was the best. I was the best. I never doubted we would succeed.'

He paused and corrected in a low voice, 'We had to succeed.'

He gritted his teeth as another spasm constricted his chest, squeezed his heart in an iron fist. 'Damn,' he muttered, clenching his fists to stop his hands from shaking.

Small, soft, cool fingers touched his face, stroked his cheeks. A gentle voice murmured comforting words.

He looked up. Caught in the light of the fire, her blonde hair formed a halo around her face and shone like the sunshine. Summer. She made him think of summer. A summer morning, filled with light and life, with the scent of wild flowers, and the promise of sweetness, life and love. Would he live long enough to see another summer?

'What happened?'

'A Sikh guard spotted us and gave the alarm,' he carried on. 'My men tried to disarm him, but failed. Other fighters arrived. We were soon outnumbered. So my men started firing. I shouted not to shoot but they didn't hear me. Shots went astray, the Sikh gunpowder magazine blew up, too early.'

He swallowed hard. 'Twenty of my men were still inside, rigging the place up with explosives.'

He rubbed his face.

'I can still hear the blast, the screams, smell the stench of burning flesh mixed with gunpowder…'

'Did the British win the battle in the end?' she asked after a moment of silence.

He nodded. 'It took two days of fierce fighting for our side to secure the victory, but casualties were high. Too high.'

Rose scooped some hot water into a tumbler, sprinkled tea leaves into it and knelt down next to him. She handed him the cup. His hands shook so much he could hardly lift it to his lips.

'You said something about your tattoo.'

He forced a few sips of hot tea down and gave her back the tumbler. He'd never told anyone about that before.

'*Ahankar* – that's Gurmukhi for pride, the cardinal evil, the worst of the five demons which plague humankind according to Sikh religious beliefs. It's my demon, my evil. I always believed I was good at what I did. Always thought I was the best.'

He let out a bitter laugh. 'I was wrong, fatally so.'

He took a few shallow breaths. Hell, even breathing hurt.

'My men died because of me. I can still hear them. I see their shadow, I feel their torment. They come for me, you know. They haunt me, every night and soon they'll take me with them.'

Suddenly the pain was back with a vengeance, its sharp nails clawing at his heart. Dizziness mind swirl and gave him the unpleasant feeling of floating away from his body.

His hand curled over his chest and he let out a moan. Perspiration beaded on his forehead, yet he didn't feel warm but cold, terribly cold as if the very centre of his being was gradually replaced by a core of ice. He started shaking.

He was dimly aware of Rose jumping to her feet, adding more wood onto the fire.

'Don't move, don't try to talk,' she said in a calm, soothing voice as she loosened his necktie and unbuttoned the top of his shirt to help him breathe more easily.

She wrapped the plaid around him and rubbed his cold hands in hers.

There was something he had to tell her now, before it was too late. Something that had been bothering him ever since his encounter with Rose's abductors.

'Listen,' he started, summoning the last of his strength, 'you must beware of Morven. I think he means you harm. The mail guard and the driver were acting on his orders when they brought you here…'

'It must be because I threatened him this morning when he was burning that village and warned him I would get him dismissed by Cameron.'

'That must be why he didn't want you to reach Westmore. Another thing… Promise you'll leave this place as soon as the storm passes, whether I'm alive or not. Take Shadow and ride west, towards Borgie.'

He winced in pain. 'Ask the innkeeper there to get a message to MacBoyd. To tell him he'll find me at *Sith Coille*. Fairy Wood.'

The last thing he saw before the shadows engulfed him was her face, pale and serious, and her huge blue eyes as she leant over him. The last thing he felt was her cool, soft hand brush his hair back then linger a moment on his cheek.

Rose stayed at his side all night. She didn't even dare close her eyes in case he needed a drink of water or tea, or if the fire went out.

In case he died while she was asleep.

He was delirious most of the time, caught, it seemed, in the never-ending nightmare of Ferozeshah, and calling endless warnings to his fallen comrades. Only once did he cry out about somebody else – a woman. He didn't say her name but repeated over and over again that she shouldn't be afraid and he wouldn't hurt her.

'I fear I'm going mad,' he said in a brief lucid moment after drifting out of yet another series of terrifying hallucinations. 'Talk to me. Please.'

So she told him about Bou Saada, and the stars shining like diamonds at night and the moon making magical shadows that moved and danced across the vast Saharan plains surrounding the oasis. She told him about the thick, moist scent of her oasis and the delicate orange-blossom fragrance – her favourite – that bathed her garden in the springtime. Her voice tense with anger and grief, she told him about the hated French army and how they'd taken her mother's estate away only the year before because of her brother's involvement with the rebels.

'Your brother was a rebel?' he asked in a weak voice.

She nodded. 'That's right. Lucas fought against the French together with his childhood friend, Ahmoud. He's given up the struggle now. He found a store of treasure last year and realised he would be more useful building roads, railway lines, schools and hospitals rather than fight a hopeless cause.'

She let out a chuckle and added. 'His main reason for leaving the rebels' camp however was Harriet, the woman he fell in love with and married last year. They're expecting a baby any time now.'

'What about his friend?'

She shrugged. 'Ahmoud is still fighting. I don't think he'll ever give up. And neither will I... I sometimes help delivering messages or giving information about the movements of the soldiers in and around Bou Saada.'

'You help? Isn't that dangerous? What does your mother say about it?'

'She doesn't know. For years she was busy running the estate, then when it was taken from us she tried to help our people survive. She's been even busier sorting the mess the French made since it was given back to us.'

Sadness and guilt tightened her throat. All this time, she'd been such a hopeless daughter, more a hindrance than a help in the estate office. Perhaps now she'd married Cameron her mother would be proud of her at last…

But McGunn wasn't listening. His eyes were closed, his breathing laboured again.

Some time before dawn she managed to coax him into getting up and lying on the bed where he would be more comfortable. He hadn't moved or made a sound since.

It was the longest, most frightening night of her life and she almost wept with relief when the first blue and grey hint of daylight filtered through a crack in the shutters. Leaving Lord McGunn's side, she walked across the room, light-headed with fatigue, and opened the door onto a white world.

The abandoned village and the forest had all but disappeared, swallowed by the howling blizzard. As she stood at the door with the icy wind whipping her cheeks, burning her eyes and taking her breath away, the reality of her predicament finally sank in.

What if the storm lasted for days, weeks even? What if they ran out of food? What if Lord McGunn died despite all her efforts? She stepped back in, closed the door against the storm and leaned against the wooden pane.

He was in a bad way, in turns feverish or shaking with cold. His heartbeat was fast and loud or so faint she could hardly feel it when she pressed her hand against his chest, and she feared he would die.

She took a deep breath. She wouldn't let him die. She would put her dislike for him aside and take care of him even if she had no idea what ailed him and all she could do was give him sips of water or warm tea, mop his forehead, or make sure he wasn't too hot or too cold.

Armed with fresh resolve, she combed her curls back with her fingers and twisted her hair into a tidy plait. Next she blew the candle out and slipped her cloak on. The flask of whisky on the table caught her eye. She took it and walked out, making sure the door was securely shut behind her.

Bruce McGunn might disagree, but that whisky was pure poison. She tipped the contents of the flask in the snow, wrinkling her nose at the smell. It must be strong to have affected Bruce McGunn so much last night. He couldn't have drunk that much, the flask was more than half-full. Well, he wouldn't drink anymore now…

She slid the empty flask into her pocket, removed the shutters from the window to let daylight flood into the cottage, then struggled through knee-deep snow towards the stables. Shadow neighed softly when she let herself in. It was the tallest, the most impressive horse she'd ever seen, much taller than the Arabians she rode at home. A little apprehensive, she reached out slowly to pat its neck before readjusting the blanket on its back. She left with the promise of returning later with a treat – an apple or two from his master's supplies.

Back in the cottage, she gathered the largest pot she could find and went out again to get water from the stream at the far end of the village. It was icy and her hands were soon red, raw and freezing. Soon her boots were wet too, her feet numb and her face stung as if pricked by thousands needles.

It was a relief to return to the house, close the door and put the heavy pot on the table. It was a greater relief still to see that Lord McGunn was still alive.

She made some hot tea then tiptoed to the bed, a steaming cup in her hand, and called his name.

He growled to leave him alone.

She ignored him.

'And how are you feeling this morning?' she asked in a bright and cheerful voice.

'Like hell,' came the muffled reply as he turned to face the wall.

'At least you're alive. Here, I made some tea.'

'I don't want anything.'

She pulled the plaid down, lay her hand on his shoulder and felt the strong, hard muscles beneath the linen shirt.

'You need to drink something.'

He turned to look at her and her throat tightened at the sight of his bloodshot eyes surrounded by dark shadows.

'You won't leave me alone until I drink that tea, will you?'

She shook her head.

'I thought so.'

48

He sat up and leant against the wall to blow gently on his tea before sipping the liquid. His shirt had come unfastened during the night and hung open on his muscular chest. Rose caught a glimpse of his oddly shaped medallion and of the blue tattoo he called his curse.

He drank the tea, and gave her the empty cup back.

'Will you go away now?'

'What about something to eat – some oat bread, an apple maybe?' She frowned, 'although you can't have them all, I did promise a couple to Shadow.'

He closed his eyes. 'All I want is to sleep. I'll be better in a couple of hours, if you can keep quiet for that long.'

'I'm only trying to help, and have a polite conversation. If you think for one minute I am enjoying being stuck in this little house with a grumpy man and a howling gale for company…'

'I don't care whether you're enjoying yourself or not. Find something to do, anything, as long as it doesn't require talking.'

She pursed her lips and stomped away from the bed.

'Never fear, Lord *McGrowl*, you shall have your wish. I'm leaving you well alone and won't utter another…'

'Rose,' he warned, softly this time.

'…word,' she finished, tossing her plait over her shoulder and trying to ignore the way her heart had flipped when he'd said her name.

After a breakfast of cheese, crumbly oat bread and tea, she searched the cottage for supplies, and couldn't repress a shriek of joy when she discovered a couple of jars filled with what looked like preserve at the back of the dresser. She opened the lid, stuck a finger inside the jam, gave it a cautious lick and smiled. It was delicious, sweet and fruity.

Unfortunately there was nothing else.

Maybe McGunn had brought more food? She emptied his bags on the table, found two dozen hard biscuits, another bag of tea, a few more small wrinkly apples and an oddly shaped, almost flat and smelly parcel she lifted out of the bag with a grimace.

'What is that stink?' she muttered, wrinkling her nose in disgust at the pungent smells of rotten seaweed, brine and salt.

She untied the thin cord, lifted the sides of the cloth and uncovered four yellowing fish fillets, no doubt carried from Wrath Harbour. She wrapped them back up quickly. She would have to be very hungry to eat them!

The other bag contained no food but a couple of changes of clothing – thick shirts, trousers, and men's undergarments she quickly tossed back into the bag – as well as a box of ammunition and a short knife in a thick, black leather scabbard. Right at the bottom of the bag her fingers touched a pair of shoes which were tucked under thick woollen socks.

She pulled them out and her eyes widened as she recognised her purple velvet slippers, the very ones she had lost in Wrath outside the Old Norse's Inn.

Thoughtful, she put them into her bag. Why had McGunn bothered to retrieve them from the village and bring them with him? The man really was surprising…

Sounds of snoring made her turn her head towards the bed. He was asleep again, but for the first time his breathing was slow and regular.

Perhaps she should saddle Shadow and ride away, straight to Cameron.

Her heart beat faster. Could she actually escape and leave McGunn on his own? She looked out of the window. Outside the storm still raged outside. Leaving now would be pure folly, especially since she didn't even know how to reach Westmore.

No, she was trapped here. At least she had a roof over her head and the cottage was warm. There was nothing else to do but rest, so she sat near the fire and closed her eyes.

Chapter Five

Rose pressed her nose against the grimy window pane. She had heard people in the clearing. Two men stood in front of the cottage, wrapped up against the cold, with hats covering their hair, scarves hiding their face from the gusts of freezing wind, and bundles tied to their back. Behind them a one-horse cart creaked to a stop. A woman climbed down and gestured towards the empty houses.

Since her cloak was still damp from the various outings she'd made during the day to fetch water and check on Shadow, Rose grabbed McGunn's black coat and slipped it on. It was far too big, of course, but at least it was warm.

'Hello,' she called, as she opened the door, shouting over the howling blizzard.

The woman let out a piercing shriek and hid behind one of the men who held out his stick and pointed it to Rose's chest.

'Put your stick down, Garbhan. Can't you see it's only a wee woman?' The other man said.

'Aye, I can see that now.' The man called Garbhan dropped his stick to the ground and pulled the scarf down from his face.

'Sorry about that, lass. I didn't mean to scare you but you startled me. I thought *Sith Coille* had been cleared by Morven and his gang last summer. I'm Garbhan McKenzie by the way, and this is my father, Angus,' he added, pointing to the old man.

The woman who had screamed peeked timidly from behind him.

'Here's my wife, Alana,' he carried on. 'And back there in the cart, there's my mother and…'

'Dad!' Two small girls and a tall, lanky lad jumped down from the cart and ran towards them.

'These three rascals are our children, Ross, Lorna and Ina.'

The McKenzie family stood facing her, with an expectant look in their eyes. Rose cleared her throat and took a deep breath.

'I am Rose,' she started, unsure of how to introduce herself. The last thing she wanted was to tell the family she was Lady McRae. God knows what they would make of her presence here alone with Lord McGunn and what awful rumours they might spread...

'Where are you travelling to in this dreadful weather?' she asked.

The friendly smile on Garbhan McKenzie's face was replaced by a glum expression.

'Inverness probably, or anywhere where we can find work and a place to live.'

Behind him, Alana let out a sob and buried her face in her hands.

'Don't start crying again, woman.' He wrapped his arm around her shoulders. 'What's done is done, and crying won't bring our house back now that Morven's thrown us out.'

Rose's heart tightened. Like so many other families in Westmore, the McKenzies had been evicted by Cameron's factor.

Garbhan gestured to the cottages.

'We heard that *Sith Coille* was abandoned and decided to stop here a day or two to sit the storm out and avoid the gangs of bully-boys roaming the roads. Drunken thugs, all employed by Morven.'

'I'll kill Morven and McRae one day for what they've done to us,' the boy growled, pulling himself up tall. 'When I'm big and all grown up, I swear I will.'

'Watch your tongue, Ross lad,' his father scolded sharply.

Shocked by the steely hatred in the boy's eyes and the determination in his voice, Rose stepped forward.

'Your father is right, young man, but don't you worry, Morven will get his comeuppance. I will tell Lord McRae about him and he'll make sure he's punished for what he's done.'

The boy narrowed his eyes, doubtful. 'Why should McRae listen to you, even if he cared?'

Her mind was made up. She would tell them her name, right this instant, and give them the assurance that they would soon get justice.

'Morven's days are numbered, I promise you. And I can assure you that Lord McRae does care and that he'll listen to what I have to say because, you see, I am his...'

'What are you doing out there in the cold, *graidheag*?' McGunn's voice interrupted, gruff and loud.

She swung round.

He stood in the doorway of the cottage. With his shirt hanging loose, his face pale and half hidden by his dark beard and framed by his long hair, he looked like he'd just got out of bed – which of course, he had. What did he think he was doing, calling her sweetheart in front of these people?

'It's freezing out there,' he added. 'Come back inside and keep my bed warm.'

What? Rose's heart stopped. Had he gone completely mad? There was no way she could tell the McKenzies she was Lady McRae now.

'Who's that?' Garbhan McKenzie frowned and pushed his children behind him.

'He is... he is...' Rose swallowed hard, unable to think of what to say next.

'I'm Bruce McGunn. Rose and I are... ahem... good friends – very good friends, in fact – aren't we, sweetie?' He winked at her.

Shock and fury rendered her speechless.

Angus McKenzie opened his eyes wide.

'You're Lord McGunn, from Wrath,' he said in a slightly trembling voice. 'We won't impose on you and your young lady, my lord. We'll leave straight away.'

Garbhan nodded and gathered his children in front of him and pushed them towards the cart.

'Don't be daft,' McGunn replied sharply. 'You can't travel in this storm, not with little ones. There are plenty of empty houses here for you to stop by tonight, but first...'

He flashed Rose another smile. 'My sweet Rose has a lovely fire going in our little cottage, so why don't you all come in and get warm? I'm sure she'll make us some tea too.'

His sweet Rose? How dare he? She would show him exactly how sweet she was feeling right now and what he could do with his tea!

'Then we accept, with heartfelt thanks.' The old man was unable to hide his relief. 'Come on, son, let's take care of the horse and unload a few supplies for tonight.'

'Will you give us a moment?' Rose asked the women in a clipped voice before stomping up to the cottage, with McGunn's coat flapping around her.

She followed him inside and slammed the door behind her. Melting snowflakes rolled down her wind-whipped cheeks, and droplets of water trickled down her neck. Her hair had worked its way out of the plait and hung, wild and tangled, around her face. In the giant coat, its sleeves well past the tips of her fingers, she probably looked half-crazed, and completely ridiculous.

She was far too angry to care.

'The fever must have addled your already weakened brain!' she started. 'How dare you let these people think we are... we are...'

'Lovers?' he suggested, arching one eyebrow. 'It's for the best, believe me. I heard what they said about being displaced by Morven and his gang. You don't really want them to find out you're married to McRae – the man who caused them to lose everything, do you?'

'For the hundredth time, these evictions have nothing to do with Cameron,' she hissed. 'They are all down to his factor.'

'You are the most mulish woman I ever met.' He crossed his arms on his chest. 'How long are you going to hide from the truth?'

'I am mulish? Well, you are pig-headed, or bear-headed, take your pick of whichever animal has the thicker skull and the smaller brain.'

His lips stretched into a slow smile. He was making fun of her. Again.

'What, you're not calling me monkey names today? I rather like it when you say I'm a macaque or a baboon.'

She clenched her fists so hard her fingernails dug into the palms of her hands. If only she could punch him! But the sleeves of his coat were so stiff she couldn't even bend her elbows.

Still smiling, he took a few steps towards her.

'What are you smirking at?' she hissed, stepping back until her bottom hit the table, with a bump. 'You don't care one jot if you just ruined my reputation, if people believe I'm your fancy woman.'

'Shh, *graidheag*, be quiet and trust me for once.'

He lifted his hand and pressed a finger to her lips. She shivered at the contact, no doubt because all she wanted right now was to bite him! His finger lingered on her mouth. She held her breath, parted her lips.

'Can we come in?' a timid voice asked as the door opened. 'I hope you're not upset because of us.'

Alana McKenzie and her mother-in-law walked in, followed by the children. The women looked at her and Lord McGunn in turns, their expression full of curiosity.

'Of course not. Please sit down near the fire. You must be frozen after travelling in the storm.' McGunn gestured towards the table and turned to Rose. 'My sweet, will you make tea for our guests while I go out to help the men? I'll need my coat...'

Seething with rage, she pressed her lips in a hard line, unfastened the coat and handed it to him.

'Thank you, *graidheag*.' He caught her hand and lifted it slowly to his lips, holding her gaze all the time as if daring her to pull out of his grip.

She could hardly slap him now, not with the two McKenzie women and the children staring, so she forced a smile as he brushed the back of her hand with his mouth. It was only a light caress but once again the contact sent shivers along her arms and back, all the way down to her bottom of her spine. She closed her eyes for a brief moment and leant towards him, almost craving more of his heat, his strength, his touch.

What was wrong with her? Her eyes flicked open, she snatched her hand away and took a step back.

A smile twitching at the corner of his mouth, he slipped his coat on, dug his hand into his pocket and pulled out something blue she didn't immediately recognise.

'By the way, I believe this belongs to you. I found it in the mail coach.'

It was her old bonnet – the one she thought she'd lost. He had found it and brought it back to her! She mumbled a thank you and snatched it from him.

'I think you should hurry before it gets dark and there's nothing left for you to do, my *graidheag*,' she said, mimicking his earlier term of endearment.

He arched his eyebrows but didn't reply. As soon as he closed the door behind him, the McKenzie children burst out laughing. Even the two women chuckled. She turned to look at them in surprise.

'What is it? Why are you laughing at me?'

'It's obvious you're not from round here, miss,' the elder girl replied, her eyes sparkling. 'You shouldn't have called him *graidheag*. That's what boys call girls. You should call him *graidhean*.'

Annoyed and still disoriented by her body's strange reaction to McGunn's kiss, Rose clutched her bonnet against her chest and pursed her lips.

'Well, I don't speak Gaelic, and right now, I can think of a few words I'd rather call him other than *McGraidhean*!'

McGorilla, for one, she thought, proceeding proceeded to list more names in her head as she added wood on the grate, hooked the cooking pot full of water above the fire and placed tumblers on the table.

Alana McKenzie sat down and looked around the cottage.

'We used to have a croft house very much like this one back in our village. Now we have nothing.' Her eyes filled with tears, her voice shook.

Her mother-in-law squeezed her hand. 'We still have one another, which is more than some folks can say.'

Remembering the two women who were burned alive in front of her very eyes the day before, Rose's resolve to see Morven punished hardened. The heartless man would pay for what he was doing to Cameron's people, she'd make sure of it. For now, she would brew some tea and offer the McKenzies a little comfort.

She opened a jar of preserve, took biscuits out of McGunn's bag and turned to the children. 'Now, I was wondering if you three were hungry.'

They clapped and cheered and wasted no time in grabbing hold of a handful of biscuits and covering them with a thick layer of jam.

'Fancy meeting Lord McGunn here!' The older woman remarked in a quiet voice as she sipped her hot tea. 'We heard so much about him. Garbhan's younger cousin was in his regiment in the Punjab, you know, and he swore Lieutenant McGunn, as he was then known, was the bravest and the most fearless man he'd ever met. No doubt you know what they used to call him.'

'The claymore devil?' Rose poured a cup for herself and sat down.

'That's right. My nephew never got over the way he was discharged for dishonourable conduct. He said it was shameful the way the other officers made a scapegoat of him, and that he took the blame for one who had deserted the field.'

Rose frowned in surprise and leant across the table.

'An officer deserted the battlefield?' McGunn hadn't said anything about that.

Alana nodded. 'Captain Frazier, he was called. He ordered his unit off the battlefield instead of charging to the aid of Lieutenant McGunn, but as he was the son of a general and had important connections he got off lightly. It was claimed he suffered from heat-stroke and didn't know what he was doing.'

She paused and sipped her tea. 'A friend of mine, a lass from the village, is a laundry maid at the big house. She said that the same Captain Frazier is a guest of Lord McRae's at Westmore Manor right now, along with a very smart crowd.'

'They must be here for Cameron's ball – I mean, for Lord McRae's birthday...' Rose sighed. 'Do you often see him...Lord McRae? I believe he takes great interest in his estate and his people.'

The women looked at her as if she'd lost her mind.

'Lord McRae? He's hardly ever at Westmore,' Alana replied. 'And when he is, he has better things to do than trouble himself with the likes of us. Of course now he's getting married to a grand lady from London, he'll be up there even less. I heard the woman hates Scotland and only agreed to come because of his Lordship's birthday ball and the reading of the banns in church.'

'What grand lady? What wedding?' Rose's hand started to shake and a little tea spilled onto the table.

'His Lordship is getting married next week. The banns were read at church on Sunday... Lady Sophia Fairbanks, she's called. Apparently, everyone at the manor house is afraid of her. She has terrible tantrums and thinks nothing of slapping her maids and throwing her fancy silver hairbrushes or silk slippers at them when the mood takes her.'

Rose tried to breathe, but her chest felt too tight and the room danced and spun around her as she rose to her feet.

Alana frowned. 'Are you not feeling well, Miss Rose? You look pale all of a sudden.'

Rose's cup shattered on the table and scalding hot tea splashed all over her dress, soaking the fabric. Her knees buckled under her and her fingers gripped the edge of the table for support.

'Miss Rose, what's wrong? Are you ill?' Alana's voice seemed far away.

'Of course, she's ill. Look at her!' The older woman scolded. 'Help me get her onto that bed over there.'

'I don't understand,' Rose said. 'Why are you saying that he's marrying some lady from London...' Panic made her heart drum in her chest, fast, too fast. 'You must be mistaken. He can't marry anybody. He just can't.'

The two McKenzie women stared at her in astonishment. The children glanced up from their jam and biscuits.

'But he is, the banns were read in church, I told you. You need to get out of that wet dress, lassie.' The old woman's tone brooked no contradiction. 'Have you any spare clothing?'

Rose shook her head. 'Only a nightdress and …' She was about to mention her pantaloons, shirt and bolero when the woman interrupted her.

'Then you shall wear your nightdress and wrap that nice thick plaid around you.' She pointed to Lord Hunter's blanket which he had left in a heap on the bed.

'No, I don't think…'

'You'd be wasting your breath arguing, Miss Rose,' Alana interrupted. 'My mother-in-law always gets her way. Besides, you will only catch a cold if you stay in your wet dress. Look, you're shaking already.'

Rose was too shocked to explain that it wasn't her wet dress that was making her shake, but what the elder McKenzie woman had just said.

Alana bent down to pick up Rose's bag. 'Come on, let's get you undressed. We'll talk later.'

Garbhan and Angus McKenzie chose one of the larger cottages for their family, and Bruce helped them unload supplies and blankets from their cart. Together they gathered wood, made a fire and tidied the place up. Like the other abandoned houses, it contained a few pieces of furniture, crockery and cooking pots, even bedding. It was as if its former occupants had left to run an errand and would return at any moment.

Bruce brought in a last pile of wood and stacked it near the fireplace to dry.

'I hope you don't mind me asking but I'm rather curious about your young lady.' Garbhan tipped the straw mattress off the bed to shake off the dust. 'She's a pretty lass but she doesn't sound like she's from round here.'

'No indeed,' Bruce replied. 'Rose is from Algeria, in North Africa.'

Garbhan let out a low whistle. 'Algeria? Now that's a coincidence. Lord McRae brought back some fancy women dancers and musicians from that very same country two weeks ago.'

He put the mattress back and stroked his chin, thoughtful. 'What's your young lady doing here?'

'Her ship was caught in a storm and had to stop in the Kyle of Wrath for repairs.' The MacKenzies didn't need to know any more.

Garbhan's father carried on pulling blankets from a one of the bags he'd unloaded and piling them up on the bed.

'I heard there were some funny goings-on in the hunting lodge with those dancers,' he said after a moment. 'Mind you, it's the same every time McRae is up at Westmore. The man is a rotten apple. He's nothing like his father. Now, he was a decent sort, Niall McRae...'

'No McRae is ever decent,' Bruce said between clenched teeth. As far as he was concerned, McRaes were, and had always been, devious, lying cheats and murderers.

'No, he was a good man, really,' the old man insisted. 'He would never have gone along with the clearances. He wanted to improve the land and life of his cottars and crofters. I remember he even wanted to put an end to the feud with your family. He visited your grandfather often. There were even rumours of...'

He stopped mid-sentence, looked away and coughed to clear his throat.

'Rumours of what?' Bruce asked, frowning.

The old man turned away, but not before Bruce saw his face colour.

'Never mind. It was a shame he got himself killed at Waterloo. Life at Westmore was never the same after that. Lady Patricia was already a harsh and bitter woman, but after Lord Niall died she let that thug Morven rule the estate like he owned it. And that son of hers, he was never any good.'

Yes, the man had got that right. Lady Patricia was indeed a heartless bitch, and McRae a depraved rake.

When the crofter's house was ready the McKenzies and Bruce made their way back to the women and children. Bruce stopped by the barn to take care of Shadow on the way. It was dark by the time he walked across the clearing. He kicked the snow off his boots against the wall, pushed the door open and was greeted by the sound of Rose's voice telling the children a story.

One glance at her was enough for his breath to catch in his throat. She sat on the bench in her long white nightdress, his plaid wrapped around her shoulders and her blonde hair falling in wild curls down to her waist, glowing like gold threads spun by fairies in the light of the fire.

The two McKenzie girls sat on her knees. Next to her the boy pretended to be bored but Bruce could tell from the intent look in his eyes that he was listening to her every word. Longing tightened his chest so much he actually stopped breathing. This was what she would look like one day, sitting with her own children – hers and McRae's children – as she told them bedtime stories.

Children… The thought of having any had never crossed his mind before. You didn't have children when you had nothing to give, nothing to teach but bitterness.

He crossed his arms on his chest and leant against the door to listen.

'And so the evil *djin* tricked Old Ibrahim to lean into the well and tugged hard on his long, black beard. Old Ibrahim fell down the deep, dark pit, never to be seen again.'

Rose paused and carried on with a whisper.

'But every so often, people swear that a long, dark shadow creeps out of the village well, slides into the houses of Ibrahim's enemies and scares them to death.'

The three children shrieked in one voice. 'The beard!'

Rose nodded and repeated. 'The beard indeed. People say it's still as beautiful, lustrous and black now as it was fifty years ago.'

Bruce smiled. A haunted beard? Now that was unusual! So this was the story behind that Ibrahim character she so often referred to.

Sensing his presence, Rose looked at him. Her face was pale, her eyes red and swollen. He frowned, a pang of alarm hit his chest.

'What's wrong?'

61

She stroked the little girls' hair before lifting them gently off her lap.

'Go and help your mother and grandmother prepare something to eat,' she said before rising to her feet.

She looked so small, vulnerable and lost that he had to fight the urge to gather her in his arms and hold her against him. Instead he pushed his hands into the pockets of his jacket and scowled.

'Why are you wearing your nightclothes when we have company?'

She pulled the sides of the plaid closer onto her chest.

'I spilled hot tea all over my dress.'

'Miss Rose got herself all upset when we told her about Lord McRae getting married,' Alana said.

'What do mean, McRae's getting married?' He glanced between the woman and Rose, who stood pale and still as a statue.

'Lord McRae is marrying a grand lady from London,' Alana explained. 'We were in church when the banns were read last Sunday.'

So Rose had lied. She wasn't married to McRae at all and McRae's wedding to Lady Sophia Fairbanks was still on... Not pausing to examine why he felt more relief than anger at the news of being taken for a fool, he took his coat off and threw it on the bed.

'I need a drink.'

'There's some tea left,' Rose said in a weak voice.

'Tea? I'd rather have a dram of whisky.' He looked around. 'Have you seen my flask anywhere?'

This time, her cheeks flushed bright pink.

'It's in your bag but...'

He arched his eyebrows. 'But what?'

'It's empty. I- I poured the whisky out.'

'You did what?'

'I thought I was doing you a favour since whisky doesn't agree with you.'

'Good grief, woman, whisky does agree with me! What happened last night had nothing to do with it,' he roared. 'Oh and never mind. If all we have is tea, then you'd better make it strong.'

Chapter Six

Bruce closed the door to the McKenzie's cottage and strode across the clearing at the centre of the abandoned hamlet. It had stopped snowing some time during the evening and the temperature had dropped even further. The cold burnt his lungs, the wind slapped his cheeks but he relished the chance to be alone at last.

He gave a last look to the cottage where children and adults were tucked up in bed, safe and warm for now. He brushed away the odd feeling he had experienced when he'd put to bed Ross McKenzie while Angus and Garbhan took care of the little girls. As the boy linked his arms around his neck and gave him a sleepy smile, he had once again felt something stir deep inside – an urge so strong, so vital and alien it had knocked him sideways. What would it feel like to have a son, to care for him, watch him grow and become a man – and to be the core of a family? Would his life have turned out any differently had he been wanted, loved and cherished like Ross McKenzie, instead of being the bastard son of a mother who'd taken her own life, the bastard grandson of a violent drunk eaten by hatred and bitterness?

He would never know… He took a deep, cold, burning breath before pushing the door to his cottage. Damn, he was being annoyingly sentimental tonight. Not a good idea when he had to confront a liar, find a murderer and save his estate from ruin.

He walked into the house and shrugged off his coat. Rose was still up, seemingly engrossed in tidying up.

He gave her a hard stare and threw the coat onto the back of a chair.

'Why did you lie to me?'

'I didn't.'

She looked calm and didn't even look at him but carried on stacking the dirty tumblers up. She then snapped shut the lid of the jam jar and brushed the crumbs off the table top into the palm of her hand. When she threw the crumbs into the fire, the flames hissed and flared.

Like his temper. He strode towards her, stopping only a couple of paces from her.

'You did lie. You heard the McKenzies...The question is why.'

The rush of heat to her cheeks didn't escape his attention, and neither did the trembling of her hands as she caught the sides of the plaid slipping off her shoulders. So she wasn't that cool and composed after all.

He narrowed his eyes, hardened his voice.

'I want answers, and I want them now. Who are you? McRae's mistress? A whore he picked up in the docks in Algiers?'

She gasped, the plaid dropped down from her shoulders onto the floor but this time she didn't seem to notice. The fire behind her outlined the contours of her body, the curve of her waist and the swell of her hips. Her blonde hair fell in tight curls and ringlets down to the small of her back, her lips parted, her breasts stretched the thin fabric of the nightdress with every breath she took. She looked as innocent as an angel, as tempting as sin.

He clenched his jaw and stepped closer. Some angel she was. She would damn well explain herself even if he had to pull the truth out of her the hard way.

'Are you even called Rose Saintclair? You may have invented the whole story about your father being a French Cuirassier colonel and your mother running an estate in North Africa.'

The post-guard's words suddenly came back to him. The man had claimed that Morven wanted to stop Rose from making trouble for McRae. What kind of trouble was he talking about? Was she planning to stop his wedding to Sophia Fairbanks?

66

'I have told no lies.' She tilted her head high and they stared at each other in silence.

Tension sizzled, so potent his body tightened, hardened, ached. His breath hitched in his throat. Blood pulsed inside him. Wife, mistress, impostor, heiress or courtesan, what did it matter? Right now he wanted her so much he didn't care who, or what, she was.

'The McKenzies made a mistake,' she added. 'Cameron can't marry this Lady Fairbanks, or anyone else, because he married me in Algiers. You must believe me. Please. I told the truth.'

Her voice broke, her shoulders rose in a helpless shrug, and tears slid down her cheeks. Something shifted, softened inside him. She sounded sincere, or she was a damned good actress.

'Let's say I believe you for a minute,' he started in a gruff voice. 'Tell me about the wedding.'

'A Reverend Thompson performed the ceremony. I'd never met him before, and neither had I met the witnesses. Cameron told me they were clerks at the Embassy.'

'Where and when did the ceremony take place?'

'In the chapel at the back of the Embassy, the evening before Cameron sailed back.'

'Hmm… Do you have the marriage certificate, the proof that you're legally Lady McRae?'

She shook he head. 'No, Cameron kept it.'

'What about your friends, can any of them vouch that the ceremony took place?'

She closed her eyes, briefly. 'Nobody came.'

'You were on your own?' He couldn't hide his surprise. 'You said Malika left after you two had an argument, but what about Akhtar, the man who escorted you to Algiers. Didn't he give you away?'

'He didn't approve of my marrying Cameron without my mother's consent – even if I was old enough to make my own decisions. He too left the day before the wedding.'

He didn't say anything but he didn't think much of this Akhtar. The man was supposed to look out for Rose, not leave alone to fend for herself and make what the biggest mistake of her life.

'So for all we know McRae could have asked someone to impersonate a minister and paid a couple of witnesses to sign a fake certificate.'

'Are you implying that my wedding was a charade?'

He shrugged. 'It seems obvious, doesn't it?'

'No, no you're wrong.' She rushed to her bag, and after a frantic search produced a small velvet pouch she opened carefully.

'Look. Cameron gave me a ring.' She held out a shiny gold wedding band.

'Anyone can buy a ring, it doesn't mean a thing.'

'But he wouldn't stoop so low as to fake a wedding. The McKenzies must have misunderstood when the banns were read.'

'The thing is, there has been talk of a wedding to Lady Fairbanks for months. That's why I was so taken aback when you arrived at Wrath and announced that you were McRae's wife.'

He softened his voice. 'The man conned you, and the sooner you accept it the better.'

'But why? Why would he do that?'

'I have no idea.' He shrugged. 'To get you into bed, perhaps.'

She let out a small whimper and fresh tears slid down her cheeks. As she lifted her hand to rub her eyes, the fabric of her nightdress brushed over her breasts again, outlining their full, soft round shape. He took a deep breath and made himself look away. A man would sorely be tempted to make up a whole heap of lies for just one night with her.

'No, it can't be, you're all wrong,' she whispered. 'Oh... What am I going to do?'

'Don't worry, things may not be so bad. I can arrange your return journey to Algiers. No one need ever know McRae took advantage of you. You could always tell Akhtar and your family that you changed your mind and did not marry McRae after all...'

When she sobbed more loudly, he clenched his fists. What an idiot. Of course! She might be pregnant and not have the luxury of pretending nothing had happened. What hadn't he thought about it before?

'Is there any chance you might be with child?' he asked.

She flung her head back as if he'd slapped her, buried her face in her hands and carried on crying without answering.

He sighed. He may have been too brusque and not have handled that the way he should have, but he hoped for her sake and that of any child that she wasn't pregnant. If she was, she would suffer the shame of being an unmarried mother, and the child would be taunted and sneered at – an outcast. Every taunt, every sneer would hurt like hell, like salt rubbed into a raw wound.

Bruce knew exactly what that felt like. Not only was he born out of wedlock, but he had no idea who his father was. His mother had taken her secret with her. All he knew was that his father was a thug and a rogue. His grandfather had said so many times – the night he announced he was enrolling him in the 92nd Gordon Highlanders for example. 'I doubt the army will make a man out of you. You're a bad seed, always were. You'll never be any good, just like your father – may Black Donald roast his balls in hell.'

As usual the memory left a bitter taste in his mouth.

He pushed it to the back of his mind, looked at the woman crying in front of him, and before he realised what he was doing, strode across the room and pulled her to him in a clumsy attempt to soothe and comfort her.

'Here. Please don't cry,' he said in a hoarse voice.

She nestled closer, and it felt like she was melting, warm and pliant in his arms. Heat shot throughout his body and suddenly he didn't want to comfort her at all, but kiss those lips and breathe in her sweet female scent until he was drunk on it.

She rubbed her wet cheek against his shirt, nestled closer and he gave up the struggle. His hands slid along her spine, rested on her waist. He bent down until his lips brushed the wet, salty velvet of her cheek, trailed down slowly towardss her mouth. He felt her tremble in his arms but she didn't move away. His hands glided further down, settled on the swell of her hips, and moulded her to him.

The feel of her smooth, naked body under the flimsy nightdress set his blood on fire. His heart drummed fast and hard. All he wanted to do was pull the gown up until he touched her bare skin, lost himself inside her and fill his darkness with her light, her warmth, her sunshine.

His fingers travelled up and down, traced feverish patterns along her spine. Her eyes still closed, she let out a helpless moan of surrender which burned through him like a firebrand. She tilted her head back, her lips parted in an irresistible offering.

No.

The word rang in his mind, loud and clear. He wouldn't take advantage of her when she was distressed and confused. Stepping away felt like the hardest thing he'd ever done.

'That's quite enough crying,' he growled. 'Pull yourself together, damn it.'

She opened her eyes and looked at him as if she'd just awakened from a dream and had no idea who he was. A fierce blush spread on her face, her throat, down to the opening of her nightdress. She took a hurried step back, picked up the plaid from the floor and covered herself with it.

'I'm s-sorry.'

'It sounds as if the worst of the storm has passed. We'll set off for Westmore tomorrow.'

'I thought you were taking me back to Wrath.'

'I changed my mind.'

She gasped. 'I see. Now you believe I'm not married to Cameron, I'm no use to you anymore. And since you can't blackmail him, you might as well take me with you and get rid of me, is that right?'

'Aye,' he answered even it is wasn't exactly true. How could he explain his sudden, irrational and overwhelming reluctance at the thought of parting with her, even for a few days? Whether she was married to McRae or not, his instincts, his whole being, screamed at him not to let her out of his sight and to keep her close to him.

Silence hung heavy between them. Then she said it was late, she was tired and was going to bed, and he pulled a chair close to the fire, sat down and prepared himself for a long vigil – and another attack of his illness.

Damn. He hadn't even thanked her for looking after him the night before. Her gentle voice, the feel of her hand on his face had soothed him, and eventually made the nightmares go away – even the dream-like vision of Malika's face, her eyes wide with blind terror and her mouth opened onto a silent scream. The same question that had haunted him for the past few days tormented him once more. Where had he seen her before? Why did she look so scared? Had he done anything to hurt the girl?

He clenched his fists on his thighs. Perhaps he would find the answers he sought at Westmore.

Rose paused at the edge of the forest. No wonder they called this place Fairy Wood. It was truly an enchanted place in an enchanted dawn which in a strange way reminded her of early morning at Bou Saada, even if snow covered the ground instead of golden sand. The sky glowed with delicate shades of violet, mauve and pinks mixed with translucent greys and blues. Further down the valley two mountains covered with pine forests and tipped with snow rose like sleepy giants standing guard. At the edge of the woods a stream sang a pure, crystalline song as it cascaded over rocks. Perhaps fairies hid behind the tall, dark firs, or behind those rocks shiny with frost and ice.

She left the path and walked across the field, her boots sinking into the pristine, thick and fluffy snow. She dropped the tin pot and dirty cups she'd brought from the cottage for washing down on the river bank, knelt down and stared into her distorted reflection.

What a sorry sight she was, with her matted hair, her eyes gritty and swollen from the lack of sleep, her face pale and blotchy. It was no wonder really, considering she had spent yet another sleepless night. This time, it wasn't Lord McGunn's illness which had kept her awake but the maddening questions swirling inside her head, over and over again. Did Cameron deceive her, and if so, why?

As she lay on the grimy straw mattress, she had replayed every moment of their three-week whirlwind courtship, culminating with Cameron proposing to her in the Jardin d'Essai one balmy evening, as stars reflected in the dark surface of the sea in the bay and a silver moon watched over them. She had dissected their wedding day hour by hour, minute by minute, to find any clues indicating that it had been a clever deception. She found none.

The evening ceremony in the chapel at the back of the British Embassy had been a little rushed because Reverend Thompson had been at the bedside of a dying British merchant all day and needed to return to the grieving family for the wake. After the ceremony, they had gone to the Excelsior Hotel, but instead of going to her room, she had sneaked into Cameron's suite in secret, since nobody was to know about the wedding. After uncorking a bottle of champagne, they'd toasted their union. He'd taken her in his arms and they'd waltzed across the room. How happy, giddy and excited she had felt!

After that everything had gone terribly wrong, which had all been her fault...

With a heavy sigh, she grabbed hold of a pebble and threw it as hard as she could into the stream. It hit a rock, bounced off and landed with a loud plop. Half a dozen ravens flew off from a nearby tree, making hoarse crowing calls which broke the perfect silence of the morning.

Why would Cameron have played such a cruel trick on her? Lord McGunn was wrong. He had to be.

She swallowed. Bruce McGunn. He was the other reason she had been awake all night.

She whispered his name and her chest tightened so much it hurt. What was it about him that made her angry and weak all at once, that filled her with longing, heat and need in a way no other man, even Cameron, ever had? He was a harsh, brutal, unpleasant man – the exact opposite of Cameron in everything – and she disliked him with a frightening intensity.

Yet she'd all but melted in his arms the evening before. Her body craved his touch, his caresses. Her heart ached and swelled up for him every time she recalled the anguished, haunted look in his eyes when he spoke of Ferozeshah and what he called his curse. Nothing made sense anymore, least of all her own feelings.

Her fingers scooped a little snow and moulded it into a ball she threw into the stream. Dipping her fingers in the water, she cupped a little icy water into her hands and washed her face until her cheeks tingled and her mind felt sharper. She rinsed out the cups, filled the tin pot with fresh water and started back towards the village just as the winter sun, a huge ball of blood-red fire, was rising between the mountains, turning the sky into a riot of fiery colours that painted the snow red and orange.

Lost in her thoughts she didn't see the beast until it was too late. It stood a few feet away only, magnificent and tall with its huge antlers and thick brownish coat. By Old Ibrahim's Beard, what was that? She'd never seen such an animal before. It was huge, and looked deadly.

For a second it seemed as unsure as herself as to what to do. Then it shook its antlers, beat the ground with its foreleg, let out a series of grunts which echoed in the silence, as if poised to charge.

A squeal of terror echoed behind her and she swirled round. The youngest McKenzie girl stood still, her eyes opened wide in fright, her face as pale as snow.

'Don't make a sound, don't move, until I tell you.' Rose willed her voice to remain calm, all the time glancing around for something she would use to make the beast go away. There was nothing which could serve as a weapon – nothing but snow. It wasn't much, but it would have to do…

Dropping the pots to the ground, barely aware of the cold water splashing all over her skirt and boots, she bent down to scoop a handful of snow. She shaped a ball and threw it at the stag's chest. The animal jerked back in surprise.

'Go back to the cottage. Now!' She told the girl before bending down to make more snowballs and throw them in rapid succession at the animal.

The stag let out a loud snort, breathed out a cloud of steam and pawed at the snowy ground. It took a couple more minutes and several more snowballs for it to turn and run away in the woods.

'Snow balls against a stag? Now that was a bloody daft idea.' A man's deep voice scolded behind her.

Annoyed, she swung round to face Bruce McGunn. His face was hard, his grey eyes almost blue in the bright morning light. Like every time he was close, her heart drummed so fast and loud she found it hard to breathe.

'I had to think of something to give the little girl time to run away.'

'It was completely irresponsible. Did you see the size of its antlers? It could have killed you both had it charged.'

There he was again, telling her off like a stupid, naughty child. Anger and hurt flooded inside her – a wild, mad torrent that made her voice shake and her face burn. She stamped her foot on the ground, grabbed hold of one of her remaining snowballs and pressed it hard between her hands until it was hard and compact.

'Well, it didn't charge, did it? What would you rather I had done? Climbed up a tree with the little girl on my back, or grabbed a stick and chased after it, or just stood there and screamed for help?'

He arched an eyebrow. 'Calm down, sweetheart, I was just...'

She stomped her foot on the ground again.

'Don't tell me to calm down, and don't tell me I am making a scene. And above all, don't call me sweetheart! I wish you'd stop talking to me as if I was five years old. I wish you'd leave me alone and I'd never see you again. But most of all I wish I'd never met you.'

'You said that before,' he remarked coolly. 'Now, if you've finished your little tantrum, it's time we went back to the cottage...'

That did it. She didn't remember raising her arm and taking aim but the next thing she knew she threw the snowball at him. It hit his chin with a soft thud.

74

She let out a squeak, put her hand in front of her mouth and stepped back.

'You need to improve your aim,' he said, deadly calm as he brushed the white powder off his dark beard. 'It was off target if you meant to get me on the nose,'

'I – I didn't mean to hit you.'

'Yes, you did. Let me show you how it's done.'

He bent down to scoop some snow and threw a snowball at her. She was so surprised she didn't move and it caught her on the shoulder.

He tossed another snowball. This time she ducked and it landed behind her.

'What are you doing?' she asked.

'I thought it was obvious. We're having a snowball fight, aren't we?'

He gathered a handful of snow, and shaped it between his hands.

'Come on, what are you waiting for?' he called, a wide smile on his face.

It took her a split second to make up her mind. If Lord McGunn challenged her to a snowball fight, then she would show him what she was capable of. She bent down, packed some snow between her hands and threw a ball but he dodged it and it landed on the ground.

'Is that the best you can do?' The sunlight caught his eyes again, made them shine with silver sparkles.

She hurled the next ball straight at his head.

'I got you! I got you!' She cried out, jumping up and down when she caught him on the nose.

'Not bad, but a little weak.'

'Weak, you said? Then how do you find this one?'

She hurled another snowball at him. It hit him hard on the chin, peppering his dark beard with white.

'That was pure chance. I wasn't concentrating. I bet you can't do that again.'

'Watch me.'

She moulded half a dozen more snowballs and pummelled him with them. Every time they hit their target with a satisfying

75

thump, she jumped up and down and shrieked with delight. In contrast, his aim was so poor he almost always missed her. It was almost as if he was doing it on purpose.

'I won! Look at you, you're all white.' She laughed as she pointed at his hair, face and coat scattered with fresh snow.

Her foot caught a rock hidden under the snow and she stumbled forward, straight into his arms, making them both lose their balance. He swayed before falling backward and cushioning their fall with his body, and she found herself lying on top of him, his body hard and warm under her.

He wrapped his arms around her, so tightly she stopped breathing, and the world became a blur – the snow fields, the dark green forest and the sharp, crisp blue sky all melted into a kaleidoscope of colours. Underneath her, he was no longer smiling, but tense and hard as steel.

He slid her up along his body until their eyes, their mouths were level. Slipping one hand onto the nape of her neck, he pulled her down towards him, slowly, inexorably. Her heart drummed as hard as a *bendir*. She held her breath, waiting, willing for their lips to touch. Her mind shut down. Nothing existed, nothing mattered but him and the flame that danced and burned inside her, higher and stronger with every heartbeat.

'Damn it, *graidheag*, I want you and I don't care who you are,' he said in a hoarse voice before pulling her down and bringing her mouth to his in a hot, rough, impatient kiss.

The thick stubble on his cheeks rubbed against her skin. It was wet with melted snow, at once soft and bristly, and made her tingle and shiver all over. She lifted a hand to the side of his face and her fingers stroked his cheek in a timid caress.

His breathing quickened, tremors shook the steely arms that pinned her to him. Pressing one hand against the back of her neck, he forced her lips open with his mouth. His tongue slid inside her mouth and he kissed her long and deep. It was like being devoured alive, possessed by an irresistible force. And vanquished.

The world exploded in millions of tiny, bright, colourful pieces and then there was only stormy darkness, waves of desire, and an unbearable heat coiling and spreading inside her.

Her hands slid along his chest and onto his shoulders and stayed there, clinging and gripping as he ravaged her mouth. More, she wanted more. She wanted him.

The sounds of voices nearby shattered the dark spell, and knocked her back to reality. She tore herself away from him, pressed her hands against his chest and pushed hard.

'Someone's coming.'

'So what?' His eyes were a dark and stormy, his breathing fast and heavy, his heart thumped so hard she could feel it against hers.

Gripped by panic, she pushed harder.

'Please. I don't want anybody to see me... to see us like this.'

He narrowed his eyes, hissed a breath and released her, and she scrambled to her feet.

'It's only Garbhan and his family,' he remarked as he got up. 'What does it matter if they see us having a tussle in the snow when they know we spent two nights alone in the cottage?'

'It matters. Of course it matters,' she cried out. Gathering her skirts, she ran blindly up the forest track. She had to escape, far away from the man who played havoc with her mind, her body... and her heart.

'Watch out, Miss Rose,' Garbhan cried out as she bumped into him. 'You look all upset and flustered. Has the stag come back to give you another fright?'

Next to him his wife and the three children looked at her with undisguised curiosity. She forced a few deep breaths down before answering.

'No, it fled into the woods.'

'We came to say goodbye,' Garbhan began, 'and to thank you for scaring that stag away. Our Lorna was so upset we couldn't make head nor tail of what she was saying. Lord McGunn was the first to understand what was happening and he shot out of the cottage. I never saw a man run as fast.'

He took hold of Rose's hand, squeezed it hard.

'There was no need for me to run,' McGunn said behind her. 'Rose was doing fine on her own. '

77

He stepped beside her, his arms filled with the tumblers and pots she had dropped near the stream, and looked at Garbhan.

'So it's agreed. I'll see you all at Wrath in a few days.'

Rose frowned. 'Wrath? I thought you were heading for Inverness.'

'Lord McGunn made us an offer we couldn't refuse,' Garbhan said with a beaming smile. 'We will be forever grateful.'

'Nonsense,' McGunn retorted. 'You're the one doing me a favour. I told you, I need more workers at the fisheries, and a couple of scullery maids at the Lodge.'

'God bless you, Lord McGunn,' Alana said, her eyes full of tears. 'I promise we'll work hard for you. You're a good man and what you're doing for us, well, it's wonderful.'

'It's no big thing. There's no need to cry,' he interrupted in a gruff voice.

Rose wasn't fooled by his harsh response. He was preserving their pride as well as saving them from life in the slums. Her breath hitched in her throat, her heart felt so tight, so full, it hurt. She felt a tug at her skirt and looked down to find the youngest McKenzie girl smiling at her.

'He looks mean but he's rather nice, isn't he?' she asked, slipping her small hand into hers and dragging her along on the patch back to the cottage. 'You must be glad he's your *graidhean*.'

'You're wrong, my dear,' Rose replied in a wistful voice. 'He's not my sweetheart.'

It didn't take long for the McKenzies to harness their horse to the cart, pile their bags and children at the back. The two women sat on the driver's seat. The men slipped their bundles onto their back, shook hands with Lord McGunn and herself and exchanged wishes for a safe journey.

When the family had disappeared down the path, McGunn walked into the cottage. He didn't talk or look at her once while they packed their bags. It was as if he had never held and kissed her, back there in the snow, as if he'd never said he wanted her, and it had all been a dream.

Her hand shook as she fastened her bag shut. Only it hadn't been a dream. It had been real, so real her lips were still swollen from the onslaught of his kiss, and she could still feel the hot imprint of his fingers on the nape of her neck.

'We're ready,' he said as he brushed the ashes off the hearth before scattering them outside.

She didn't answer but watched him shutter the windows and secure the door. Once again, the cottage stood empty and abandoned. She sighed.

'What's wrong?' He glared down at her. 'Aren't you glad we're leaving this place?'

'Of course I'm glad. I can't wait to be in Westmore and prove you wrong about Cameron.'

She adjusted her bonnet and tied the ribbons under her chin.

'You'll have your chance tomorrow. We should get there just in time for your grand ball.' He looked down. 'And then you'll get your wish.'

'What wish?' She frowned.

'You will be back with McRae and never have to lay eyes on me again.'

He was right. That was exactly what she wanted, so why did the thought suddenly make her want to cry?

Chapter Seven

Rose squinted against the sunlight that bounced and sparkled on the surface of the sea. The white seabirds with black-tipped wings Lord McGunn had called kittiwakes and gannets glided on the wind in an endless dance, their strident cries rising above the roaring waves. Gusts of wind whipped strands of hair out of her bonnet and around her face, seeped through her clothes like icy fingers and left a salty taste on her lips.

The ground shook as white-crested waves charged against the cliffs, hit the rocks with such force sea spray flew high in the air, then retreated as if to gather strength, only to move forward again. It was awesome, and exhilarating. It was magnificent.

'You're cold.' McGunn wrapped his arms more tightly around her.

She stiffened. 'I'm fine.'

How could she tell him that the shivers coursing through her had nothing to do with the freezing wind and everything to do with him? His muscular thighs encased her body, his scent mingled with that of the ocean. Every time she breathed she felt the hard wall of his chest against her back, and remembered how it had felt to lie on top of him when he'd kissed her.

'We should be in Porthaven by late afternoon,' he remarked as he guided Shadow along the cliff path. 'Tomorrow we'll ride to Westmore Manor, a few hours away from there.'

She stared at the snow-covered moors which stretched as far as the eye could see and shook her head.

'I had no idea Cameron's estate was so vast.'

'Half of it used to be ours before the McRaes stole it.'

Remembering what Cameron had told her about the long, embittered feud between McRaes and McGunns, she frowned.

'I thought your ancestor Fergus McGunn was to blame for the loss of the land. He joined the Jacobite rebels and that's why his lands were confiscated and given to the McRaes who had remained loyal to the king.'

Bruce McGunn reined Shadow in and looked down, and she suddenly felt a little nervous about the steely glare in his eyes, the way his jaw had locked and the silence that stretched between them for what felt like long minutes.

'It is true that unlike most clans chiefs from the northern Highlands, Fergus fought for the Stuarts' cause,' he said at last. 'He had managed to survive Culloden and was travelling back to Wrath with what was left of his men when Gordon McRae and his men intercepted him. McRae had him beaten him up and dragged him to London in shackles. He was executed on Tower Hill. After that, McRae was rewarded by the King with a large chunk of our family estate.'

He paused. 'McRae's actions had nothing to do with being loyal to the king and everything to do with revenge. By having Fergus executed, he killed two birds with one stone, so to speak. Not only did he get the lands his family had coveted for generations, but he took his revenge on Fergus for snatching his fiancée from him.'

'Snatching his fiancée?' Cameron hadn't told Rose anything about that.

McGunn nodded. 'A few years before, Fergus had captured her ship as it sailed around Cape Wrath. He took her hostage and asked McRae for a ransom.'

Her eyes widened. That story sounded strangely familiar.

'McRae paid up, Fergus returned the ship but kept the woman.' A brief smile touched McGunn's lips and sparkles of silver lit his eyes.

'You mean he kept her a prisoner?'

'Not at all. She came to her senses and realised she'd rather marry a McGunn than a McRae.'

'The poor woman probably never had a choice. What became of her after Fergus was executed?'

'On his way back from London, McRae lay siege to the Lodge and demanded that she marry him now she was a widow, but instead of giving in, Noelie threw herself from the top of the tower, leaving her son behind – my grandfather.'

His eyes darkened and she wondered if he was thinking about his own mother.

'Anyway,' he started again, 'some claim she still haunts Wrath Lodge.'

'The Dark Lady,' Rose said in a whisper.

Was Noelie the lonely presence lurking in the shadows at Wrath Lodge, the shadow of the woman she'd spoken to and followed around the castle – and the one who'd left the sprig of pine she still carried in her pocket? After all, Noelie was French, and the woman did have a French accent.

A shiver crept down her spine. By Old Ibrahim's beard, she'd spoken to a ghost! She looked up. 'You've seen her, haven't you?'

Lord McGunn turned his grey gaze towards the line of the horizon.

'No, of course not. It's just a story.'

'Lord McGunn, you are a liar. You *have* seen her, many times probably. If she's just a fabrication as you claim, then how do you explain this?'

She slipped her hand into her dress pocket and pulled out the posy.

He glanced at it and lifted his eyebrows. 'What's this supposed to be?'

'A very old bouquet that she left in front of my door the very evening I arrived at Wrath Lodge.'

He shrugged. 'It must have fallen from someone's pocket.'

She tutted and put the posy back into her pocket. Insisting was pointless, he'd never admit she was right and he was wrong.

'The music box belonged to her, didn't it?'

He gave a brief nod. 'Fergus had it made in Paris as a wedding present – 'My Fair Love's Lament' was Noelie's favourite tune. It was my mother's too. She used to play it to make me fall asleep at night, or so I was told. It's been broken ever since she died.'

'It's not broken. I heard the music.'

83

He glared at her. 'You must have imagined it.'

His voice was so sharp she didn't dare argue this time.

'Anyway,' he went on after a short silence. 'It's a damned shame Fergus didn't pass on the secret of the rebel gold before he died.'

'What gold?'

'The gold King Louis of France despatched for Charles Stuart. After their ship ran aground, the Jacobites threw part of it in Lochan Hakel but a few rebels escaped to Balnakeil with the rest. I can't tell you how long and hard I searched for it when I was a lad. I explored every cave, every derelict bothy and ruined *caisteal* I came across, but never found anything.'

He took a deep breath.

'I could certainly do with it right now. If McRae and his bankers don't respond to my... ahem... arguments, I'll have to put the fisheries and most of my land up for sale at auction to repay the loans my fool of grandfather had the bad judgement to contract.'

She frowned. 'I thought you said I was no use to you any longer since you don't believe I am married.'

'I still have the *Sea Eagle*. It's a brand new clipper. I'm sure McRae won't want anything to happen to it whilst it's undergoing repairs at Wrath.'

'You wouldn't destroy the ship, would you?'

The cold resolve in his eyes was the only answer she needed.

'I'll do anything in my power to save Wrath from McRae's greedy clutches,' he said. 'Anything.' He stared ahead and dug his heels into Shadow's sides to urge him on the path.

They didn't speak again until they reached Porthaven. As she watched the landscape unfold – the bare, rocky cliff top to one side and the majestic, snow-covered mountains to the other – Rose couldn't stop thinking about poor Noelie and Bonnie McGunn.

Both women were linked not only by the way they'd died, but somehow by the music box too, that same music box which played for her even though it was supposed to be broken.

There must be a simple explanation for it. The clock's mechanism had probably got jammed and somehow Rose had unstuck it when she handled the clock that very first night at Wrath Lodge.

Nothing, however, explained the woman in the black cloak – the Dark Lady. A shiver of unease ran along her spine. Like many natives of North Africa, she believed that djinoun inhabited the vast Saharan plains, rocky canyons or secret springs, and enjoyed stories about the antics of mischievous spirits like Old Ibrahim's haunted black beard. But to have spoken with a real ghost was altogether different. Was it Noelie who had whispered in her ear on the night of the Northern Lights and urged her to rescue Bruce from the cliff top, or had that been just a dream?

The sunset was setting the sky and the sea on fire when they reached Porthaven at last. Lord McGunn slowed Shadow to a walking pace to negotiate their way through the hustle and bustle of the main street where market traders dismantled their stalls and piled carts high with tools, utensils and crates of food.

Shadow skirted sideways as a red-cheeked woman threw a bucket of water nearby to wash off fish carcasses and Rose had to hide her face in the folds of her cloak to avoid gagging at the stench. Further down, poultry clucked in wicker cages, dogs barked, and children ran across the street holding scraps of food they'd snatched.

McGunn stopped in front of an inn opposite the square.

'We're staying here tonight,' he announced before climbing down.

He held out his arms to help Rose to the ground, and once again her face heated up and her heart did that annoying thump and flip when his hands encircled her waist and she slid down along him. Thankfully he didn't seem to notice. Slinging the bags over his shoulder, he handed Shadow over to a stable boy and strode into the inn with her in tow.

'You're in luck, Lord McGunn,' the innkeeper said after checking his ledger. 'We do have two rooms left for tonight, which is unusual, it being a market day. What's the young lady's name?'

'Rose Saintclair,' McGunn answered.

'You'll be glad you chose my establishment,' the innkeeper said, his face flushed with pride as he wrote their names inside his book. 'The Nag's Head is the most comfortable in town, that's why the mail coach always stops here on the way to Thurso... although we didn't see them this week.'

'Really? Any idea why?' McGunn asked in a casual voice.

'Apparently the storm brought a tree down on the main road, they had to do a detour and skip Porthaven. At least that's what Effie told us. She's one of my serving women and the coach driver's cousin... Anyhow, we'll get you and the young lady settled right away. Supper is at six. Don't be late down, it'll be busy. It's *ceilidh* night.'

Rose glanced at McGunn, expecting him to tell the man about the mail guard's and coach driver's attempt at abduction, but he didn't say anything.

'Effie! Come here,' the innkeeper called. He shook his head and let out a loud sigh. 'That lass does nothing but look at herself in the mirror and gossip all day.'

'About time, I had all but given up on you,' he scolded when a pretty red-haired woman strolled into the lobby. He ordered her to have hot water and bath tubs brought to Lord McGunn's and Rose's rooms at once.

'Please excuse me now, my Lord. I have deliveries to attend to but Effie will be able to help with anything you need.' The innkeeper hurried away to a back room.

'Let me know if you need any assistance for bathing, my laird,' the maid said in a husky voice as soon as the landlord was out of earshot. 'I am often complimented about my soft, capable hands.'

She lay her fingers onto his forearm and gave a little squeeze.

Rose fully expecting Lord McGunn to put the brazen girl back in her place with a gruff word or a stern look but all he did was smile.

'I don't doubt it for a moment. Yours are lovely hands indeed.'

Rose had heard him so pleasant. Was he feverish?

'Thank you, my lord.' The maid handed him the room keys. 'I shall see you later then.'

'I'll look forward to it.' He flashed her a smile, slid the keys into his pocket and picked up the bags. 'For now, I need to take Miss Saintclair to her room.'

Rose followed him, her back stiff, her lips pursed in an angry scowl and an odd and bitter sensation twisting her insides.

'I don't need you to carry my bag or take me to my room,' she snapped as they started up the stairs. 'Especially when it's obvious you have more pressing things to do, like sweet-talking a serving girl. It's funny how you've changed into Lord McGracious all of a sudden; I hardly recognise you.'

What was wrong with her? Her voice sounded sour, her chest felt tight and painful, silly tears stung her eyes…

He must be wondering the same thing because he turned towards her and arched his eyebrows. Furious with him, and even more furious with herself, she stared straight ahead and pressed her lips together.

Once upstairs, he took a key out of his pocket and stopped in front of a door at the end of the corridor. He slid the key into the lock and pushed the door open.

'I believe this is your room. The landlord said it was the largest and the quietest.'

He walked in and lifted her bag onto a chair. 'It's a little more comfortable than *Sith Coille*, isn't it?'

Walking to the door, he added. 'By the way, I want you to stay in your room tonight. I'd rather not attract too much attention. I'll ask the maid to bring up some food for you.'

'Would that be before or after she scrubs your back with her lovely soft hands?'

As soon as the words were out, her face heated up, her breath caught in her throat and she bit her lip, hard. Bedbugs! What had she said that for? She sounded like a shrew, mean, bitter and jealous.

'Who scrubs my back is no business of yours, sweetheart.' He cocked his head to one side and a smile curled the corners of his mouth. 'Unless you volunteer your services, of course.'

'Don't be ridiculous.' Shame constricted her chest and her throat, making it impossible for her to breathe.

'Then I'll see you in the morning.' Still smiling, he let himself out.

At last, Rose drew in a long breath. She pressed her hands to her hot cheeks. Why did the man always bring out the worst in her, and make her look stupid and unreasonable? Anyone would think she was jealous when it was the honest truth she didn't care a jolt if the maid jumped in McGunn's bath and they both drowned in it together!

She looked around the room, this time taking in the thick green curtains already drawn against the night but which she would open later, the fire burning high in the fireplace and thick woollen rugs on the floor which gave the room a cosy, welcoming feel. The furniture was sparse but the large bed was piled high with blankets, and the mattress so soft she all but sank in when she sat down.

'By Old Ibrahim's beard, now this is what I call a bed.'

How nice it would feel to slip under the covers and lay her head on the fluffy white pillows instead of the grimy, scratchy straw mattress at *Sith Coille* or the cold, lumpy bed at Wrath Lodge.

There was a knock on the door and three manservants came in, carrying a small bath tub they proceeded to fill with buckets of hot water. A proper bath, at last. It was weeks since she'd had one. Forgetting her bad mood for a moment, she laced the water with a good measure of her orange-flower cologne, slipped out of her filthy clothes and stepped into the hot, fragrant water.

After scrubbing herself clean and washing her hair, she reclined against the tub and let out a sigh. If only she could erase the last few days and pretend they were nothing but a bad dream and return to the way she felt on the *Sea Eagle*, when all she was concerned about was to prove she wasn't just a scatterbrain, make her mother and brother proud, and be the wife Cameron wanted.

Now everything had changed. Her best friend had been murdered in the most horrific circumstances. She didn't know what was real or not. She didn't even know what she felt. Yes, she sighed. Everything had changed when the *Sea Eagle* was caught in a storm and she'd met Lord McGunn.

She gripped the sides of the bath and closed her eyes. Why couldn't she forget about the man, even for five minutes? Just thinking about him – his eyes forever changing from storm clouds to sparkling silver, his mouth which tightened in a stern line or curled in a seductive smile in a heartbeat – was enough to make her pulse race and give her goose bumps. His mouth…

Her eyes flicked open. She didn't want to think about his mouth, or the way he'd kissed her that morning. She didn't want to remember how his touch always set her senses ablaze. She didn't want to think about him at all!

She sat up, gathered her hair to one side and twisted it to wring the water out. One more day and she would be rid of his infuriating, overbearing presence. She would never have to listen to his lies about Cameron duping her into a fake marriage or trying to ruin him, or about him being responsible for all these poor people being evicted and made homeless.

No, she would never have to see him again, and wasn't she glad about that!

One more day and she would be with Cameron…

She tried to conjure an image of her husband's bright blue eyes and easy smile, but all she seemed to be able to remember was the heated flush on his face as he ripped her nightdress open, the harshness in his voice as he ordered her to touch him… A lump grew in her throat, preventing her from breathing, an iron fist squeezed her stomach. It was as if her whole body contracted at the memory of his hands groping at her breasts and between her legs, pushing his fingers inside her until she implored him to stop. And then driving into her, relentless, despite her cries.

She had to forget about that night. Cameron had drunk too much champagne, and her immature, frigid response had made him angry and impatient. The next time would be different, better, that's what he'd said. She swallowed hard, pressed a hand to her heart. The next time…

She took a few calming breaths. Everything would be fine. She was nervous about seeing Cameron again, that was all. It was only to be expected, especially since they hadn't parted on good terms in Algiers.

There was also the matter of Morven. Cameron might not believe her when she told him about the atrocities the man he considered a family friend was committing in his name. And, of course, she would meet Cameron's formidable mother, Lady Patricia, and be formally introduced as Lady McRae at the ball. It was enough to make anyone anxious.

She grabbed a bath sheet to wrap herself in and stepped out of the tub. She took her time drying in front of the fireplace. Soon the crackling and hissing of the burning logs, the repetitive movement of the brush through her hair soothed her. Enticing smells of roast meat, warm bread and soup now drifted into the room from the dining room below and made her stomach growl.

Where was that silly maid who was supposed to bring her food? Too busy taking care of McGunn, probably. Never mind, she would get her supper herself. She picked her clothes from the floor and pulled a face when smells of damp and horse wafted from the stained, crumpled fabric. Her stockings and undergarments were in dire need of a wash too, and her spare blue dress was just as bad. The thought of putting any of them back on now she was clean was bad enough, but the idea of presenting herself the following day to Cameron and his mother wearing dirty, smelly clothes made her shudder.

She would wash the whole lot right away. The undergarments were easy to deal with. She dipped them into the bath, washed them thoroughly and hung them to dry on the back of a chair near the fireplace. The dresses were another matter. All she could do was to scrub the worst of the stains off and freshen them up.

When she was finished, she had nothing to wear but her pantaloons, her white shirt and black bolero, and the purple slippers Lord McGunm had retrieved for her.

She followed the sounds of laughter and conversation and soon found herself standing in the doorway of a tap room. The air was thick with tobacco smoke and the smell of hot food, ale and whisky. The noisy crowd was mostly male, with a few women's dresses adding a touch of colour here and there. Rose tilted her head up and took a few tentative steps into the room.

'I don't believe this,' a black-haired giant of a man bellowed in a thick, drunken voice. 'Look who's here. One of McRae's harlots, just for me.'

He let out a booming laugh and Rose froze as voices died down and she was faced with all heads turned towards her.

The big man set his half-empty pint of ale on the counter and approached. She stepped back but he grabbed hold of her wrist and pulled her inside the room.

'Come and have a drink with me, my lovely. Then I'll take you home and you'll give me a private performance. I heard things about you and the way you make men wild.'

Panic made her heart race. She pulled back as hard as she could but the man was too strong.

'Leave me alone! You have no idea who I am, you have no idea...'

He swirled round to stare at her, arched his bushy black eyebrows and grinned, uncovering several stumps of yellowed teeth.

'Ooh, so you speak English, unlike your little friends. Come to think of it, you don't look quite as exotic as them...' He shrugged. 'Never mind, I bet you're just as good.'

Still holding her wrist, he took his pint and brought the glass to her lips to force her to drink. Her teeth clattered on the glass and she coughed as beer swished down her throat. Around them several men cheered, although Rose also heard a few calls to release her and leave her alone.

'Let the lady go.'

Rose almost went limp with relief. Never had she been so happy to hear McGunn's voice.

The man put his pint down and turned to face him.

'Lady?' He laughed coarsely. 'She's no lady. She's one of the hussies McRae keeps in his hunting lodge for his pleasure, well out of sight from his stuck-up fiancée.'

'What fiancée?' Rose let out a strangled cry.

The man laughed. 'That English bitch, Lady Sophia. The woman orders us around as if she already owns the place. The truth is, she's as ugly as a rat's arse, so it's no wonder McRae spends his time chasing petticoats in all the villages on the estate or bedding his dancers.'

His hand clasped around Rose's waist, he bent down to nuzzle her neck. She was too stunned, too weak suddenly to fight him off. So the McKenzies were right. McGunn was right. Cameron had lied. He was getting married to another.

'For the last time,' McGunn called again, 'I'm asking you to leave the lady alone.'

The man snorted. 'If you want her, you'll have to fight me for her.'

McGunn narrowed his eyes. 'That's not a problem.'

Calmly, he unfastened the buttons of his black jacket, shrugged it off and threw it on the back of a chair. Next he rolled up the sleeves of his white shirt to his elbows.

'What are you waiting for? I'm hungry and my stew's getting cold.'

Her throat tight with dread, Rose glanced up at the big man still holding her. He was as tall as McGunn, but looked a lot bulkier and meaner. His nose was bent to one side, a long scar barred one side of his face, and his hands were huge and rough, with grazed knuckles as if he'd recently been in a fight.

He looked down at her. 'This won't take long, my lovely.' He gave her bottom a squeeze, pushed her aside and lunged at McGunn.

He was right. It didn't take long.

McGunn's first punch hit him squarely on the nose, the second in the stomach. The man doubled over, fell to his knees with a grunt, and collapsed on the floorboards. He remained there, eyes closed, snuffling loudly through his bloodied nose.

McGunn picked his jacket up and slid it back on.

'Get him out of here,' he ordered a couple of men before looking sternly at Rose. 'Come with me.'

In silence she followed him to a table tucked away in a corner of the room. A half-full pint of ale stood next to a steaming plate of stew and a thick slab of bread.

He pulled a chair out. 'Sit.'

She did as he said.

'I told you I didn't want to attract attention, and you come down here dressed like… that.' His eyes narrowed to slits. 'Why didn't you stay in your room?'

'I was hungry. The maid didn't come to bring any food.'

'Ah.' He sighed and looked a little contrite. 'That was probably my fault. She came to my room earlier. We started… ahem… talking and I forgot to ask her to bring you a tray.'

She heaved a breath and clasped her hands together under the table.

'I see.'

Her brain must be completely muddled because right now the thought of him cavorting with the red-haired maid hurt even more than having her worst fears confirmed about Cameron.

He pushed the plate of stew and his fork in front of her.

'I'll tell you about it later. For now, you'd better eat while it's hot.'

She tilted her chin up.

'I don't want to know about your frolicking with the maid, thank you very much, and I couldn't possibly eat anything. You heard that horrid man at the bar. The McKenzies were right. You were right. Cameron is going to marry this Lady Fairbanks.'

Her voice broke. 'How stupid I have been. He did deceive me after all.'

'It seems that way.'

She expected him to gloat or at least smile with the satisfaction of having been right all along, but the only thing she saw on his face was concern. He pointed to the plate.

'You're exhausted and you've had a nasty shock. You need to eat.'

Protesting once again felt useless. Reluctantly and with a shaky hand she took hold of the fork, speared a piece of mutton and brought it to her mouth. It was a little tough but she forced herself to chew and swallow it, then she ate some more. Chunks of melt-in-the-mouth carrots and tasty turnips followed, and before she knew it, she had eaten almost half the stew.

'That's better.' Lord McGunn slid the pint of beer in her direction. 'Now have a drink.'

She took a few sips. The bitter ale made her wince. She may not like whisky, she liked beer even less.

'There's something I really need to know,' he said as she put the glass down. 'I asked you before but you didn't answer. Why did McRae leave you behind the day after your pretend wedding instead of taking you with him on the *Sea Lady*?'

Rose's heart tightened. If there was one thing she didn't want to talk about, and with him especially, it was her wedding night. However, from the determined glint in his eyes, it was clear he wouldn't give up until he had answers. Perhaps she could tell him some of the truth.

'We had an argument.'

He arched his eyebrows. 'What about?'

She swallowed hard. 'My father's diary, mainly.'

'I don't understand…'

'He wanted it, there and then, but I couldn't give it to him because I had put it in my mother's safe at the Banque d'Algérie a few days earlier, after my hotel room was broken into.'

She paused to take a long breath.

'Cameron was so angry when I told him he would have to wait until the bank reopened he stormed out and only came back the following morning. That's when he announced he was sailing back to Scotland. He asked me to retrieve the journal and wait for the *Sea Eagle* to come for me.'

'Why the rush? He could have waited until the bank opened.'

So she would have to confess to her inadequacies after all…Bending her head, she spoke very quickly. 'I think he was annoyed with me for… Well, for not being the wife he'd expected and… he wanted to teach me a lesson. At least, that's what he said.'

McGunn did not say a word but stared at her for a long time. What was he thinking? That she was a hopeless fool, probably.

After a while, he finished his ale and put his empty glass down.

'Well, sweetheart, there's only one thing to do now. I need to see that diary, and since I don't speak French, you're going to have to read it to me.'

Chapter Eight

'You want to read my father's diary? Why?'

Bruce sat back on his chair and crossed his arms on his chest.

'Because I'm intrigued. Lady Patricia sent her precious son all the way to Algiers just to read it…'

'Oh no,' Rose interrupted. 'Cameron didn't just want to read it, he wanted to buy it. He offered me a ridiculous sum of money to tear out the pages relating to his father and give them to him and was quite put out when I refused. I made it clear that were he to offer a thousand gold Napoleons, I would never sell the diary, not even a page, because I promised my mother to look after it.'

Blood drained from her face.

'My mother…She'll never forgive me when she finds out what I've done.' She let out a sigh and shook her head. 'I always was a disappointment to her, to everybody in fact, and once again I have proved how stupid I am…'

A tear rolled down her cheek. This time, the compulsion to touch her was too strong. Leaning across the table, he lifted his hand to her face to catch the transparent pearl with his finger as it reached the side of her mouth – that soft, yielding mouth he burned to taste again. His body tightened in a raw, primitive response, his breathing quickened. As if she felt the need inside him, her eyes widened and she pulled back.

'Don't blame yourself too much,' he said, his voice a little hoarse. 'McRae is a consummate liar and a scoundrel. You were naïve and easy to fool.'

She stared at him. 'You have a real way with words, Lord McGunn. You just made me feel a lot better.'

'I only meant…'

'I know exactly what you meant, and for once I agree with you. I was completely taken in by Cameron's flowery words. All my friends knew he was just pretending, that it was impossible a man like him should fall in love with me and want to marry me, but I only heard what I wanted to hear and believed what I wanted to believe. I was a fool indeed.'

Her lips quivered, and her eyes swam with tears which she quickly wiped away with the back of her hand.

'I am deeply ashamed for having been so stupid.'

He banged his fist on the table, so hard the glass and the plate jumped up and startled her.

'If anyone should be ashamed, it's McRae for lying to you and for… ahem… whatever else he's done to you.'

He swallowed hard. God knew the idea of McRae's hands on her slender body, of his mouth on her skin, knotted his gut in a fist and made angry, red hot flashes flare in front of his eyes.

'So what about that diary?' he resumed gruffly. 'Why do you think the McRaes, mother and son, are so interested in it?'

'I told you already, it's because my father wrote about the night he spent at Niall McRae's deathbed after Quatre-Bras and the instructions he left him.'

'What instructions?'

'About his last will and testament.'

He whistled between his teeth. 'Now that's interesting. How did McRae react when he read the diary?'

'The first time Cameron read the entries about his father, he was shaking so much he couldn't even turn the pages properly. I had to prise the diary from him for fear he would inadvertently rip pages out.'

She frowned.

'The second time wasn't much better either. I'd left him alone to give him the privacy he requested, but I realised I'd forgotten my parasol and returned into the room. I found him kneeling next to the fireplace, trying to rescue the diary from the fire where he'd inadvertently dropped it.'

'A fire?'

'He said he was overcome by a great chill while reading the diary and had to make a fire. When the diary dropped into the

98

flames, he was so shocked he didn't even think of using the tongs! Thankfully I was quick-witted or the diary would have been lost there and then.'

Bruce shook his head. McRae had inadvertently dropped the diary into the fire? His hands shook so much he almost ripped pages off? The woman was really too naive for her own good.

'You mentioned that your hotel room was burgled,' he remembered.

She nodded. 'Twice in a week! The manager of the Excelsior was mortified, and so apologetic. He said it'd never happened before and couldn't understand how the burglars had gone past the security guards in the lobby. He suggested they might have had some inside help... Anyway, thankfully nothing of any value was stolen. The first time the thieves took a few trinkets I had left on my dressing table. The second time, they emptied my travel trunks, pulled out the desk drawers and had strewn all my papers around but left with nothing.'

She sighed. 'The hotel manager wanted to call the gendarmes but Cameron refused categorically. He said he couldn't possibly have my name – and his – mixed up in a scandal. He was staying at the Excelsior too, you see.'

'Where was the diary?'

'After the first burglary I hid it under a loose floor tile on the terrace,' she answered with a tight smile. 'But after the second, I decided to store it in my mother's safe at the Banque d'Algérie.'

'So yours was the only room broken into...'

'That I know of.' She narrowed her eyes. 'Why do you ask?'

'No reason, I'm just curious.'

It seemed clear that McRae was somehow behind all this. What if McRae had commissioned the burglaries after failing to destroy – or buy – the diary? When the thieves had been unable to locate the document, he had gone through the charade of courting and marrying Rose. He must have expected her to hand over the diary during their wedding night, for him to destroy once and for all. Then he would have sailed back on the *Sea Lady*. Alone. He had been away from Scotland, and Lady Fairbanks, for too long. The date of his real wedding was fast approaching, the banns had to be read and preparations had to be made, so it was imperative he returned to Westmore.

Still, what were a few more days when he had been away several weeks already? He could have gone with Rose when the bank reopened.

No, he thought, raking his fingers in his hair, something had happened that night, something that had prompted his hurried departure.

'I think we'll take a look at that diary now,' he started, but his words were drowned in the strong, regular beat of a *bodhrán*. A lively fiddle tune followed and several couples took place on the dance floor. The *ceilidh* had started.

Rose turned to him, a smile on her lips and her eyes shining like stars.

'What beautiful music, it makes me want to dance too!'

It was as if all her sorrows, all her worries, had vanished with the first notes of the fiddle. An overwhelming feeling swept through him, fierce like a winter gale. He wanted to see her smile this way again. Every day. Nothing mattered at that moment but to make sure she was safe and happy, whatever the cost.

He was being ridiculous. He had never felt like this before, about anyone. Hell, he didn't want to feel this way ever. So he'd taken a fancy to a woman…it wasn't the first time and it wouldn't be the last. He couldn't afford being distracted by Rose or anyone else, not when he had his estate to save from ruin, and a killer to catch, and a riddle to solve. And that Saintclair diary was a riddle indeed.

He rose to his feet. 'We're not here to dance or listen to music. We've wasted enough of the evening already. Let's go and read that diary of yours.'

A familiar voice called his name across the crowded room and stopped him in his tracks.

'Lieutenant McGunn!'

He turned, frowned as he scanned the crowd and broke into a smile at the sight of the tall, fair-haired and solidly built man waving and striding across the room.

'Wallace! What the devil are you doing here?' Bruce clasped the man's hands in his and gave him a slap on the back.

'I could ask you the same question, Lieutenant. You're a fair way from Wrath.'

Bruce nodded. 'I have some business to attend to in Westmore.'

'Westmore? Don't tell me you're invited to McRae's engagement ball.'

'No, but I need to see the man about a rather sordid and complicated affair.'

'Isn't it always when that scoundrel is concerned?' Wallace retorted with a shrug of his powerful shoulders.

'What about you? I thought you were still in India. When did you come back?'

'Three months ago. I didn't re-enlist when my time was up. My father died last year and my mother can't cope on the farm on her own, so I came back to help. Actually there are a few of us who are back home. The lads will be well jealous when I tell them I bumped into you.'

His weather-beaten face suddenly creased into a broad grin and he shook his head.

'It's good to see you, Lieutenant. Let me buy you a pint of ale or a dram of whisky.'

Bruce's chest constricted. 'You know I don't have any right to be called Lieutenant, not anymore.'

Wallace waved his large hand.

'That's rubbish. The men and I always knew who was to blame for what happened at Ferozeshah. It was damned unfair you were made to carry the can for that poltroon of Frazier. If he hadn't run away, we would have mounted a diversion and our men would have rigged the depot before it exploded.'

Bruce's heart seemed to stop a second, his throat tightened. 'What's done is done,' he said in a low voice. Whatever Wallace or anybody said, the ultimate responsibility for his unit lay with him. He had failed his men, and that's all there was to it.

'Will you have that drink with me?' Wallace asked again.

Bruce snapped out of his dark thoughts and forced a smile.

'I will, but I'm buying. First let me introduce you to Rose Saintclair, the young lady I'm travelling with.'

He gestured towards the table where Rose sat, her eyes riveted on the musicians and the dancers.

Wallace opened his eyes wide and let out a curse.

'She looks beautiful, just like a princess from a fairytale. Who is she?'

Bruce couldn't repress a smile. 'I didn't know you read fairytales, Wallace. Come, I'll introduce you.'

After brief introductions, Wallace pulled a chair to sit down and Bruce made his way to the bar. It was busy so it took him a while to get served. As he pushed his way back into the room, carrying two pints of ale and a small glass of sherry for Rose, the noise level seemed to suddenly increase. The music became louder, faster. The crowd cheered, clapped and tapped their feet on the wooden floor.

What was happening back there? And where the hell were Rose and Wallace?

He put the drinks on their table, scanned the room and let out a resounding curse. Sure enough, there they were, dancing in the middle of the floor as if they didn't have a care in the world.

Had Wallace gone mad, and Rose taken leave of her senses? Had she already forgotten what trouble she'd narrowly avoided by showing up in her exotic costume only an hour before? She must have asked Wallace to dance and the big fool had probably been too dazzled by her smile to refuse.

He stuck his hands in his pockets and leant against a wooden post to watch. Rose's cheeks were flushed a deep pink, her eyes glinted with pure happiness. Her lips parted in a breathless smile at she swirled at Wallace's arm. Her blonde hair caught the light as it skimmed past her waist and bounced onto the swell of her hips.

Her feet hardly touched the ground and she looked about to fly straight into Wallace's arms, which judging by the wide grin on his former sergeant's face, he wouldn't mind at all. Not surprising, he thought with a pang of longing, a man would do anything to have a woman look at him like that. No, he corrected. A man would do anything to have *this woman* look at him like that.

Was it only six days ago that she had come into his life, blown into his winter by the *gailleann?* Wallace was right. She was a princess, a fairytale creature from a sunny, faraway land, a woman whose very scent drove him insane. Right now, it felt like he had known her, desired her, ached for her all his life. He let out a ragged breath and turned away. He had no right to feel that way. No right at all.

As he started back to his table, his attention was drawn to a man standing near the entrance. Even though he had his back to him, there was something familiar in the way he stood, his shoulders hunched in his thick brown coat, his dark hair flicking in his thick neck under a grey woolly cap. Bruce narrowed his eyes. Strange, he looked just like his man McNeil…

But McNeil was in Alltacaillich, miles away from here.

An unwelcome thought sprung into his mind. Perhaps McNeil had come looking for him because there'd been an accident at the fisheries, or trouble in the village, or again because Morag had taken a turn for the worse. Yet how would McNeil know where to find him?

As he pushed his way through the dense crowd he caught another glimpse of the man. This time there was no doubt. It was indeed McNeil. He called out and waved, but McNeil didn't hear and by the time he reached the doorway, he had left.

He couldn't have gone that far, Bruce thought as he swung open the door of the tavern to go after him. Cold, sharp air stung his face and burned his lungs. Only a misty, blurred crescent of moon and a couple of gas lights lit the night. He put the collar of his jacket up, pushed his hands into his pockets and left the hazy lights, the music and noise of the inn behind. A hundred feet away from the tavern, the streets were quiet and dark. Where had the man disappeared to?

As he started down a cobbled lane leading to the harbour, instinct made him pat the side where he usually carried his pistol. Damn. He'd left it in his room at the inn. A noise behind him resounded in the empty lane. He froze and looked over his shoulder. A cat darted along the wall and melted into the shadows. He carried on along the quays, stepping over empty baskets and coiled ropes, and walking around piles of fishing nets.

A dozen fishing boats, all empty, danced on the surf, their masts clanking in the breeze. The sea appeared black with only a few curls of silver where the moonlight touched its surface. Smells of seaweed and rotting fish filled the air, waves lapped at the jetty and the harbour wall.

McNeil wasn't here. Nobody was. He was wasting his time.

Suddenly the hair at the back of his neck prickled. Sounds of rapid footfall behind him echoed in the silence. He spun round, just in time to see the huge shadow of a man lunge at him. A fist connected with his face, hard enough to slam his head back. Stunned, he fell to his knees with a grunt. Before he could scramble up to his feet, another man kicked him hard in the stomach.

One of the men grabbed hold of his arms, twisted them behind his back while the other punched him again, knocking the air out of him. He groaned, tasted the metallic tang of blood. The man holding him let go suddenly and he slumped down, his face scrapping the slimy, wet cobbles.

'He may be a devil with a claymore, but without it he fights like a sissy,' his attacker sneered.

Bruce caught his breath. He recognised that voice. It was the mail-guard.

'Got your knife?' the other asked in a harsh whisper. 'Good. Finish him off while I go after the woman. She's the one Morven wants. He wasn't happy when you messed up at *Sith Coille*.'

'We didn't mess up,' the guard retorted, indignant. 'Everything was going to plan when *he* got in the way. Now I've lost my job, and if McGunn reports me for abducting the woman, I'll probably hang. Anyhow, the woman'll be easy to deal with once this bastard's dead.'

Bruce tensed up. A dark, hot knot of rage twisted and grew inside him. So it was true. The mail-guard worked for Morven. But what did Cameron's factor want with Rose? Whatever it was, these two thugs wouldn't get rid of him so easily, and they certainly wouldn't touch a single of Rose's hair, not as long as he had a breath of life inside him.

With a mighty roar, he leapt to his feet, tackled the man closest to him and brought him down. He straddled him, punched him in the face. There was a sickening sound of bone crushing under his fist and the man stopped struggling.

Bruce sprang up just in time to see the mail-guard pull a knife out of his pocket. The blade glinted in the pale moonlight. Hunching forward, he shifted on his feet, ready to pounce.

Bruce didn't give him time. He grabbed hold of his wrist, punched him hard in the stomach then kneed him in the groin before prising the knife out of his hand. It fell on the cobbles with a clinking sound. He then smashed his fist into the man's face in a single, powerful blow.

The guard stumbled, fell on his back with a loud thump and lay sprawled on the cobbles, grunting and spitting blood.

'What do you want with Rose Saintclair?' Bruce asked, pushed the tip of his boot onto his throat.

'Don't know what ye mean,' the man wheezed.

Bruce bent down and twisted his fist into the man's collar. Lifting him up at arm's length, he slammed him against the wall of a cottage. The moonlight was just bright enough for him to see his attacker's features.

Small, beady eyes deeply set under thick, dark eyebrows stared back at him.

'Why did you lock her up in that house at *Sith Coille*? And why is Morven interested in her? Answer, damn it, or I'll finish you and your friend right now.'

His arm ached. His head ached, hell, his whole body ached. He wouldn't be able to pin the man against the wall for much longer.

The man's eyes opened wider and stared at something beyond Bruce's shoulder.

Bruce glanced back and let out a curse.

Two tall, dark figures stood behind him, both armed with clubs. They were upon him before he could step aside. Blows rained on his head and back, flashes of light exploded in front of his eyes. His last thought before he slipped into unconsciousness was that he could have sworn he'd heard these men's voices before – in Inverness, the night he and McNeil were attacked on the docks.

'I wonder where my Lieutenant is.' Wallace scanned the room, empty now the *ceilidh* had ended. 'Something's not right. He bought us drinks then disappeared, but that was over an hour ago.'

'He may have gone for a walk, or to meet someone.' Rose frowned. Her cheeks burned and she added, 'There is this red-haired serving girl he seems to like rather a lot…'

'A girl? Somehow I don't think he'd go dallying with a lass and leave you here with me,' Wallace protested, an indignant look on his face. 'No, something's up and I…'

'Good Heavens, Lord McGunn!' The landlord's voice resounded in the hallway, interrupting him. 'Look at the state of you! Did you have an accident?'

'He's back.' Wallace rose to his feet but Rose was faster.

Pushing past him, she darted towards the hallway, so fast that she tripped on a mat and fell straight into McGunn's arms.

'Watch what you're doing, woman!' He winced in pain as he caught her. 'I don't need any more bruises.'

She gasped as she took in the blood trickling from a cut to his forehead, the contusions on his cheekbone, and his swollen left eye.

'By Old Ibrahim's Beard, you're hurt!' She disentangled herself from his grasp but stomped on his foot as she moved aside.

'Oops. S-sorry.'

He scowled at her and hissed between clenched teeth.

'Why is it that you happily trample all over me but never once stepped on Wallace's feet when you two were twirling on the dance floor earlier?'

'Whatever happened, Lieutenant?' Wallace asked.

'I was set upon by a gang at the harbour. My fault, entirely. I was careless, I didn't even take my pistol. It could have been far worse had an old fisherman not come out of his cottage and raised the alarm.'

'What were you doing there?'

Wincing, McGunn walked across the lobby to lean against the counter. 'I thought I saw one of my men in here and went looking for him. I didn't find him, I must have been mistaken.'

He paused. 'Listen, Wallace, I need to speak to you, and make plans for tomorrow. Can you stay a while longer while I take Rose to her room and tidy myself up?'

Wallace nodded. 'Of course. I'm stopping at my uncle's tonight. You remember him, don't you? The man's an owl, he never goes to bed before dawn. He won't mind if I come back late.'

He gestured towards the counter. 'I'll get us a couple of whiskies while I'm waiting.'

'Good man.'

McGunn asked the innkeeper for warm water and fresh towels to be brought up to his room then turned to Rose.

'Come with me,' he ordered as he took hold of her elbow to march her up the stairs.

Although she didn't care for his tone or his iron grip on her arm, she didn't protest. Somehow she knew it would be pointless.

'Make sure you lock you room up tonight,' he said when he opened her door, 'and don't open for anyone else but me.'

'Why?'

'The men who attacked me were after you. One of them is the mail-guard. He's working for Morven.'

'Are you sure? What would Morven want with me?'

'I don't know,' McGunn said in a low voice. 'But I intend to find out.'

Chapter Nine

Rose pulled the curtains half open onto the night so that she could see the sky from the bed. Even if the crescent of moon was thin, pale and blurred, and only a few stars pricked the sky's velvety darkness, it was still better than being closed in. She set the oil lamp on the bedside table to adjust the light. The flame hissed and flickered in the yellow tinted globe, making huge shadows on the wall.

Holding her father's diary against her chest, she slid under the bedcovers, shivering as her bare feet made contact with the cold sheets. She gave the fluffy pillows a tap and sat back with the diary on her lap. Her fingers stroked the leather binding and traced the burn marks and charred edges caused by Cameron dropping it into the fireplace. Inside, the pages were yellowed and brittle. Soon it would fall apart, the ink would fade, and there would be nothing left of her father.

No, that wasn't true. She would always have the memories of his smile, of the intense blue of his eyes, of the warm, solid feel of his arms around her, and the deep rumbling of his voice. She closed her eyes and smiled. She would never forget his voice. She still heard it in dream sometimes. It always sounded so real it was as if he was right there, next to her, like the evening she was locked inside the abandoned cottage at *Sith Coille*, scared and cold before Lord McGunn arrived.

The journal slipped from her fingers. She had forgotten all about that strange dream until then. Her father had pointed to the diary and urged her to find a medal. What medal? He did write about a medal in his journal, but it was Niall McRae's medal… Never mind, she sighed, it had only been a dream.

She opened the diary again and flicked through the pages until she found the first entry about her father's encounter with Captain Niall McRae.

'*16th June 1815…*' she whispered. '*Quatre-Bras.*'

'*21:30. What a terrible mess today's been, what a wasted opportunity! As the murky daylight gave way to a moonless night, putting an end to the fighting, we realised we'd lost every inch of ground we had managed to gain earlier today. So many dead and wounded and it was all for nothing! Now we have pitched our tents in the mud and struggled to light fires under the rain, it is time to tend to the wounded – ours and a few dozen English, Scots and Dutch we have brought from the battlefield to the hospital tent. We might have lost the battle today but we made a substantial number of prisoners, although what we're supposed to do with them, I have no idea.*

All kinds of rumours are flying around the smoky camp fires tonight, rumours that make the men angry and bitter. The worse by far is that our enemies stripped our fallen cuirassier comrades naked and left them to rot in the mud, and now Wellington's and Blücher's troops are eating their dinners from their breastplates.

Victory should have been ours – it was ours, if only for an hour or so, before the debacle, and now we're all wondering what the hell went wrong. Why did it take so long for Ney to issue the orders to take Quatre-Bras, and why did d'Erlon's First Corp spend the afternoon marching between Quatre-Bras and Ligny?'

She carried on reading, her lips moving in a whisper.

'*22:30. Back from a tour of the camp. Ney just left with his aide-de-camps and I can hear Kellerman rant and rave in his tent nearby. He has good reason to, he only narrowly escaped death after Ney's daring – some said suicidal – charge. When his horse was killed under him, he rode away standing on the stirrups of two of his cuirassiers.*

In the hospital tent the chaplain, who doesn't speak a word of English, asked me to talk to a Scottish captain from the 92nd Highlanders regiment, a Lieutenant Niall McRae. Ever since he regained consciousness after the battle the man has been begging for a scribe to write his last will and testament. The chaplain says he won't last the night. McRae is in terrible pain and yet he shows great courage. He is a brave devil, I'll grant you that. I hope I'll have his resilience when my time comes.

Something strange happened when I first lay my eyes on him. I had the most peculiar feeling I knew him, yet I'm sure I've never seen the man. Even though he is lying down on a stretcher, I can see how strong and tall he is – a real force of nature. The man's a fighter. The laudanum the surgeon gave him for the pain didn't do much to knock him out. He won't take anymore because he wants to keep a clear mind to dictate his letters before it's too late.'

A knock on the door broke the silence and made Rose jump.

'Rose? Open up, it's McGunn.'

She drew in a sharp breath and put the diary on the bedcovers next to her.

He knocked again. 'I want to talk to you.'

'Just a minute, I'm coming,' she answered, jumping out of bed and frantically looking for her shawl.

She gave up the search when he knocked a third time, a little harder. At this rate he would wake up every single patron in the inn. She unlocked the door and opened it just enough to peer through. He had changed into a fresh white shirt, washed the blood off his face and combed his hair back. His eye was still slightly swollen but the cuts and bruises didn't look quite so bad now.

'What took you so long?' he grumbled. 'I thought we agreed you would read me your father's diary.'

'I didn't think you would still want to, not after what happened.'

He shrugged. 'I told you, I'm fine. Aren't you going to let me in?'

She didn't have much choice, so she opened the door. As soon as he walked in the room felt too small, hot and stuffy. Painfully aware of her state of undress, she glanced around and let out a small whimper as she spotted her freshly-washed stockings and drawers dangling from the back of a chair at the side of the fireplace.

'Just let me tidy those away,' she stammered as she rushed to the fireplace to pull her undergarments down and throw them in a heap on the floor.

He looked at the bed, the covers down and the pillows still bearing the imprint of her body, then at the window and his face hardened.

'Why the hell did you leave the curtains open? Anybody can see you from the square. I told you these men were after you.'

'Oh… I didn't think. You're right, of course. It's just that I have this… thing about dark, confined spaces, and I can't breathe if I don't see the sky, the stars, the moonlight.'

He arched his eyebrow. 'You're afraid of the dark.'

She grimaced and gave a brief nod.

'You never complained when we were at *Sith Coille*.'

'You were there, so I wasn't afraid.'

'Well, I'm here now too and I don't want to risk anybody seeing you from the street and finding out which room you're in.'

He walked to the window and drew the green curtains with a sharp tug.

'Sorry I'm so late, but the maid took her time bringing hot water and towels, and then I had to talk to Wallace.'

'The maid?' she said in a sour voice. 'I hope her soft hands didn't disappoint.'

He frowned. 'What are you talking about?'

Embarrassed, she shook her head.

'Nothing. Just forget it. What you do with chambermaids is none of my business. I shouldn't have said anything.'

He seemed to think for a moment, then he drew in a long breath.

'I was only trying to sweet-talk the girl into telling me about her cousin's whereabouts – the mail-coach driver. Poor Effie is most upset with him because he ran away to Inverness yesterday having taken her all her savings. No one in her family understands why he left his work for the Royal Mail. They all think he's gone mad…Of course, I found out tonight at my own costs that if the driver ran away, the mail-guard is still around, and is in fact in league with Morven and they are trying to prevent you from reaching Westmore.'

He pulled a chair and sat down near the fire, stretching his long legs in front of him.

'Let's get on with that diary, shall we?'

She nodded, picked the diary up she'd left on the bed and sat opposite him to read the first entry once again, translating it into English as she went along. Every time she looked up, he was staring straight at her, sharp and intense, absorbing her every word.

Her hand shook a little as she turned the page.

17th June. 3:30am

Captain McRae died twenty minutes ago. I stayed with him until the end. It was odd that I should feel the man's death so keenly. It wasn't the first time I saw a man die from battle wounds – God knows I killed enough men myself – but there was something about him, something I can't explain, a connection of some kind. I guess I'm just being fanciful. It's probably because I'm so damned tired.

The question is, what do I do now? I can't go to my superiors since they wouldn't give a damn about McRae's last will and testament, and riding to the 92nd Highlanders camp is out of the question. So I guess I have to wait and keep the three letters I wrote on McRae's behalf safe in my greatcoat bag until I can dispatch them to Scotland when the campaign is over. I don't know what good it'll do, though. I don't share McRae's faith in human nature. Pride and greed too often take precedence over justice and fairness. In the case of Niall McRae and his son, I fear this is exactly what will happen.

As well as the letters, McRae also entrusted me with his personal effects. There isn't much. A monogrammed silk handkerchief embroidered with heraldic griffins, a silver whisky flask, a pair of fine leather gloves and a particularly fascinating item I didn't immediately recognise - one half of a gold medal, the Order of the Crescent, granted by Selim III, ruler of the Golden Porte, to British officers after the Anglo-Ottoman victory at the 1801 battle of Canope.

McRae had it cut in half, so that only half the moon crescent, the star and sunrays remained, as well as the first two digits of the date. The man said he gave the other half to his woman, and begged me to send his own back to her, together with one of the letters.'

Rose lowered the diary on her lap.

'By Old Ibrahim's Beard... I think my father just described your medallion.'

McGunn sat up, looking pale and tense. 'It seems like it,' he said at last.

'But... how did it come to be in your possession?'

'I have no idea. I was told it belonged to my mother. It passed onto me after she died. Please carry on.'

'I have to skip a few pages. Two days after Quatre-Bras, on June 18th, it was of course...'

'Waterloo,' he finished.

'That's right. The next time my father mentions Niall McRae is on 22nd June. After Waterloo, my father followed Napoleon's retreat to Paris where he witnessed the Emperor's abdication in favour of his son.'

'L'Elysée, 22nd June 1815

We're camping at the palace, and despite the tents and campfires on the grounds and the garrisons standing guard at the gates, the atmosphere is quiet and subdued. There was no sign of Napoleon today. The word is that he is preparing to leave for La Malmaison to plan his next move – not that he has an awful lot of choices. It won't be long before Wellington, Blücher and their armies are at Paris' gates. According to the latest reports the Prussians are already marching towards us, destroying villages and crops on their way.

I haven't been able to dispatch McRae's letters and personal effects to Scotland yet. I keep thinking about the man's anguish that last night, and of his determination to make sure his woman and child were provided for. I hope I won't fail him.

L'Elysée, 27th June 1815

The Emperor left for La Malmaison. We are now left to our own devices and waiting for the allied forces to enter the capital. I have resolved to travel to Scotland and deliver the letters in person as soon as I am discharged from my duties.'

'Your father came all the way to Westmore?' Bruce asked, startled.

Rose flicked through a few pages and shook her head.

'No. He was entrusted with an important mission in the following weeks and chose one of his men, a Capitaine Raymond Pichet, to take the letters in his place.'

She flicked through the diary and put her finger on a page.

'Ah, here it is...'

'Paris, 2nd August 1815

Captain Pichet came for his orders today. He's a good man and I trust him to fulfil his duties with efficiency and integrity. I revealed only the bare minimum of McRae's story, enough for him to understand the importance of his mission but not enough to jeopardise the necessary secrecy surrounding McRae's family circumstances.

I advised him to start with McRae's lawyers in Inverness – Longford and Stewart– where he should hand in the will I scribed and witnessed at Quatre-Bras, as well as McRae's personal effects and the letter to his wife. He should then travel north to deliver the last missive. He promised to keep me informed of developments by writing to the French consulate in Algiers where I have now been assigned.'

'There were three letters,' Lord McGunn remarked. 'One to the lawyers, the other to Lady Patricia... Who was the last letter addressed to and did Pichet succeed in his mission?'

'My father didn't write the name of the recipient of the last letter,' Rose replied, 'and poor Capitaine Pichet was murdered in Scotland at the end of August. My father only heard of it a few months later.'

'Algiers, 15th October 1815.

I received some sad news today. Pichet was mugged and killed in Scotland, but the details of his death are still unclear, according to the report the local police sent the French consul in London. The poor man appeared to have been robbed, beaten up and left to die on a stretch of moorland near Kinbrace, north of Inverness.

It took some time to establish his identity because his bag with all his papers was missing and he was wearing civilian clothing. He was eventually identified thanks to his regimental signet ring which was tucked inside his coat pocket and the tenacity of a Scottish police constable who got in touch with our War Office.

Since I don't know if Pichet managed to deliver all of McRae's letters and personal effects, I thought it best to write to the lawyers to introduce myself, relate the circumstances of my meeting with their late client and relay his last wishes all over again, especially regarding his child and the woman McRae loved so much.'

'I wonder who this person was, and why my father didn't write their name.'

'Keep reading,' was all McGunn said.

'*Algiers, 30th November 1815.*

'*Still no news from Scotland. Have written to the lawyers again. Losing patience now. Told them I will visit them in Scotland myself if I do not receive a reply soon.*

Algiers, 10th January 1816

Have received at last a brief letter from Langford and Stewart assuring me that they did meet with Captain Pichet at the end of August and followed the instructions left by Niall McRae regarding his estate and last will and testament. They also write that they gave Lady Patricia her own letter and her late husband's personal effects. It's a great relief to me to learn that MacRae's last wishes were fulfilled. May he now rest in peace.'

'Is that it?' McGunn's voice was hoarse.

She shook her head.

'No, there is something else. A few months later, my father received a report from the French consul in London about the enquiry regarding Pichet's death.'

'It is dated March 1816 but my father didn't get his copy until the summer.'

'*Algiers, August 15th 1816*

I received this morning a copy of the report sub-inspector MacLellan from the sheriff's office in Inverness sent the French

116

Consul in London regarding Captain Pichet's death. It seems all loose ends have finally been tied and that Pichet's killer was apprehended and punished for his crime. I feel saddened and angry that Pichet died carrying out my orders. It should have been me travelling on that lonely stretch of road that day.

I attach the report below.

Inverness, 8th March 1816

To Colonel Hugo Saintclair, care of His Excellency René Eustace d'Osmond, French ambassador to London

Sir,

You wished to be kept informed of developments in the enquiry into Captain Auguste Pichet's murder which occurred near Kinbrace at the end of August 1815. My initial investigation pointed to the killing having been carried out by a group of vagrant soldiers recently discharged from their regiment and who had since been causing trouble in the area on numerous occasions.

I wasn't very hopeful of apprehending the gang until I came across new evidence pointing to the culpability of a certain Donald Robertson. A former private in the 92nd Gordon Highlanders from the parish of Tongue, Robertson was arrested after a brawl in a Thurso tavern four weeks ago, during which he stabbed a man to death.

The weapon he used was a four-inch folding knife with the following inscription carved on the bone handle: '2ème cuirassiers, toujours'. A search of Robertson' person and belongings produced the sum of three pounds and ten Napoleons. At first Robertson refused to explain how the above came to be in his possession, but he later confessed to taking part in the ambush and the killing of the French man.

As he was charged with murder he claimed to have been instructed to carry out the attack on Pichet by a 'person of high distinction and status' whom he promised to name at his trial. It was all lies of course. Robertson was a thief and a murderer without scruples or conscience, who had made so many enemies he got himself stabbed to death in his cell the day before his trial.

117

I hope you will find that justice has been done in the case of Captain Pichet. I remain at your service should you require further information.

> *Yours faithfully,*
> *Sub-Inspector McLellan'*

The room became dark and cold, almost as cold as his heart. He swallowed hard, and pushed a long gulp of air into his lungs.

He closed his eyes as a memory he thought he had managed to forget flashed into his mind. It was summer. He was sixteen years old and on leave from the military academy and was caught one evening by one of his grandfather's men getting a little too familiar with the blacksmith's daughter. The man sent the girl home and dragged him, barefoot with his shirt hanging out of his breeches, all the way back to the Lodge and his grandfather's study where Doughall had given Bruce a resounding slap.

'I thought the army would teach you how to be a man of honour,' he had said, seething with anger. 'I should have known you'd be too much like your no-good father. In fact, not only do you look more like me with every passing day, but you are following in his footsteps and proving eager to sow your bad seed and produce your own bastard children, just like he was.'

His eyes had narrowed to slits, hardly visible under his bushy grey eyebrows. His face flushed bright red with rage and drink, he had spat one last insult. 'The man dishonoured your mother, brought her nothing but misery. He killed her, as surely as if he had pushed her off that cliff himself.'

Pointing to his medallion he added, 'Get rid of it. That's the only thing your father ever gave your mother. Can't imagine how a man like him got hold of it in the first place. He probably stole it…'

So his drunk of a grandfather had been right after all. The great mystery of his birth had been cleared up, thanks to Rose Saintclair and her father's diary. At long last he knew who is father was.

Donald Robertson. A vagrant soldier. A murderer.

Chapter Ten

'That's all there is about my father's involvement with Niall McRae.'

Rose closed the diary and let it drop onto her knees.

Lord McGunn sat still and silent, with his eyes closed. Shadows danced on his face, emphasised his cuts and bruises, the tight lines around his mouth and his dark beard. He hardly seemed to be breathing yet the air sizzled with tension around him.

'Could I possibly take a look at... Would you let me...?' She bit her lip.

His eyes flicked open. With the flames from the fire reflecting in their gunpowder grey, they were like windows onto a wild, stormy soul.

'Let you do what?' he asked sharply.

She swallowed hard and took a step forward.

'Take a look at your medallion. I want to see if it is indeed Niall McRae's.'

'Who else's could it be? I don't think there are many Battle of Alexandria medals cut in half, do you?'

He let out a bitter laugh and unfastened the top buttons of his shirt. Tugging sharply on the medallion, he yanked it from his neck and held it out.

'Here, keep it if you want. I certainly don't want it anymore.'

She closed the gap between them and reached out for the medal. It was still warm from his skin. With trembling fingers, she traced the outline of the moon crescent, of the half star next to it and the sunrays all around. She had noticed the two numbers before '18'. No doubt the other half bore the numbers '01'.

'I wonder how your mother came to have it.'

His eyes narrowed, his face hardened.

'I think it's obvious. Donald Robertson gave it to her after killing Pichet, probably as some kind of love token. At least now I know who I really am. The bastard son of a murderer.'

'No, that can't be true,' she protested weakly, even though she'd had that same thought too.

He rose to his feet and closed his hand around her fingers and gripped so hard the medal's ragged edges dug into her skin. She gasped and he immediately loosened his grip, but did not release her hand.

He snorted. 'There you are. It seems you were right all along about me being a thug and a brute. Hardly surprising really, considering who my father was.'

'You're not a thug or a brute!' Her throat was suddenly too tight to speak, her heart filled with a feeling so powerful it took her breath away. 'And even if you do happen to be Donald Robertson's son, it doesn't mean that you are like him in any way.'

'Doesn't it? My grandfather used to say I was a bad seed. He even called me the devil's spawn whilst in one of his drunken rages. Now I understand why, and I can't say I blame him.'

'Well, he was wrong.' Her cheeks were hot, her breathing uneven. 'How can you say you're evil when you care so much about your people, about the families evicted by Morven and the men who served under you in the Punjab? You're a good man, Bruce McGunn, I know you are.'

He arched his eyebrows and the ghost of a smile appeared on his lips.

'You're not exactly a good judge of character, are you, *graigheag*?'

'Well, I...' She bent her head. What could she say? He was right, at least as far as Cameron was concerned. She had been naive and easily taken by appearances and lies. But this was different. *He* was different.

'Anyway,' she started again, unable to understand why she cared so much about him all of a sudden, 'even if you are... who you think you are... there are still a few things that remain

120

unexplained, like who that third letter was addressed to, for example.'

Faced by Bruce's stubborn silence, she carried on.

'And why Cameron and Lady Patricia want my father's diary so badly.'

'I don't know.' He shrugged. 'Perhaps they want to blackmail me, use it to force me out of Wrath once and for all.'

He took the medallion from her.

'Well, that won't happen. The only thing that connects me to Robertson is this wretched medal.'

With one sweeping gesture, he threw it aside, towards the fireplace. It made a clanking sound when it hit the cast-iron fireguard.

'What are you doing? It was your mother's, you must keep it.'

She started towards the fireplace, but he still held her and he yanked her back towards him.

'Leave the damned thing alone. It makes me sick just thinking I wore it all these years.'

He lifted her hand to his mouth and slowly, brushed his lips against the red lines the medal had cut into her palm. Shivers coursed along her arms, down her spine, as heat gathered and spread inside her.

'I'm sorry I hurt you.'

He looked down, and in his eyes was so much pain and darkness her heart ached. On an impulse she stood on her tiptoes and kissed the side of his mouth. It was only a light, gentle kiss meant to comfort and soothe, but his whole body shuddered under her touch.

He let out a low, almost savage growl and his arms flew around her waist. Tugging on her hair, he tilted her face up and kissed her with the urgency and raw need of a starving man. His mouth tasted faintly of whisky as he parted her lips open and took possession, in turn soft and hard, demanding and tender. It was hotter, darker, a thousand times more potent than the kiss he'd given her that morning – so potent she slumped, limp as a rag doll in his arms.

His hands spanned the width of her waist. He stroked the small of her back, slow and insistent, hot enough to sear her skin through the thin fabric of her nightdress. All she heard was the gallop of her heart, their fast, ragged breathing and the rustle of their clothing as they moved against each other. Once again all she felt in his arms was the overwhelming desire to touch and be touched, to love and be loved.

She brought her hands up to his shoulders and clung for support whilst his fingers raked through her hair and brushed it aside. He bent down to trail slow kisses along the curve of her neck, from her earlobe to her shoulder, and then back again. She wriggled and sighed as the heat of his breath tickled, the stubble on his cheeks scraped her skin, and the pressure of his lips created tremors at very core of her being.

Her lips parted on a shallow breath as his hands slid past the opening of her nightdress, and cupped her breasts through the fabric. She hardly noticed it when she threw her head back and arched against him, seeking the pressure, the heat, the hardness of his body. When he started rubbing his thumbs over her nipples, in a slow, insistent caress, a flash of heat pierced right through her. Her legs trembled and buckled under her, and she let out a soft, hoarse moan he stifled with a kiss.

Still holding her tightly, he stumbled back into the armchair, pulled her down into his lap and cradled her in his arms. The scent of his skin, the erratic drumming of his heart echoing her own made her weak and dizzy.

He said something in Gaelic – something wild, rough and tender all at once that she didn't understand – kissed her mouth again, and took her into the heart of the storm. His fingers traced slow, feverish patterns along her throat, over her breasts until they felt full and tight, and strained against the fabric of her nightdress. None too gently, he pulled the nightdress down and trailed kisses along her throat, on the soft swelling of her breasts, while caressing the inside of her thighs, in long, feathery strokes. And when his mouth closed on a nipple, and his tongue teased and aroused, she could only bite her lip hard to repress a moan.

Her body filled with aches and needs that coiled, twisted and grew inside her – an explosion of sensations, a chaos of desires and torment. There wasn't a coherent thought in her mind, yet she knew with blinding clarity that what she felt right now was more than the physical urge to touch and be touched.

It was the overwhelming need to be his. It was the strongest, brightest and most wonderful feeling in the world – as intense and dazzling as the Sahara sun.

She loved him.

How could she not have understood it before? She nestled closer and slid her hand into the opening of his shirt. She needed to touch him, feel his heartbeat under her fingertips. His arms were taut bands of steel around her, hard and strong, yet she felt them tremble when she stroked his bare chest and traced the outline of the tattoo he called his curse.

His arms, his whole body tensed. He moved back, and with a shaky hand rolled her nightdress back up to cover her up.

'It's late.' His voice was gruff. Under the palm of her hand, his heart beat fast, too fast.

Hers felt like it was shattering into a thousand pieces.

'I must leave you to get some rest.'

Gently he pulled her hand away from his chest, lifted her off his lap and rose to his feet. A fierce, merciless pain clawed at her heart. He didn't want her. She all but gave herself to him and he couldn't wait to get away.

Pressing a hand against her mouth, she turned towards the fireplace. Suddenly he was there, right behind her. He put his hands on her shoulders and spun her around.

'Rose, *graidheag...*'

Unable to meet his gaze, she stared down at her bare feet but he slid his thumb under her chin. His grey eyes bore deep into hers. There was heat, and kindness, and something else – something that looked like pain.

'I'm sorry. I took advantage. It was unforgivable.'

His voice was low, so low she could hardly hear.

'For a moment, I forgot everything. I forgot who I was, and I forgot the whole damned world around us. It was wrong. It shouldn't have happened.'

She didn't answer. She couldn't speak even if she tried. Her lips were still swollen from his kisses, her body tingled from his caresses, her heart filled with love and longing for him, and he said it had all been a terrible mistake.

He let go of her and stepped back.

'You should get some sleep. I've arranged for Wallace to come over early in the morning and take you to his farm.'

She flinched. Her breath caught in her throat.

'His farm? I don't understand. You said I would go to Westmore with you.'

He shook his head. 'It was before I knew Morven and his thugs were after you. You'll be safer with Wallace.'

So he wanted her as far away from him as possible.

'I told you I wanted to see Cameron, and speak to him.'

He narrowed his eyes. 'Do you still harbour any illusions that you are married to him and that he's going to announce your wedding at the ball?' There wasn't a trace of kindness now on his face, in his voice. 'Believe me sweetheart, you aren't. He may have bedded you but it's Lady Sophia and her money he's marrying, and begging him won't make a blind bit of difference.'

She shook her head. 'No, you don't understand. I want to…'

'The sooner you accept McRae deceived you, the better,' he cut in.

She stomped her bare foot on the floor. 'Bedbugs and stinky camels! Will you let me explain?'

His face stony, he opened the door. 'There's no need for you to explain anything. You've said enough. Now make sure you lock up after me and keep these curtains closed.'

And after a last, scorching look, he walked out and shut the door behind him.

The sound echoed into the room, and into Rose's heart, hard and final.

'I don't want Cameron, I don't love him,' she whispered in the empty room. 'I love you.'

The sound of his footsteps decreased in the corridor. There were a couple of odd thudding noises and a door slammed shut.

Perhaps she should go after him, try to explain once again why she had to go to Westmore.

She didn't move. There was no point. He made it clear he didn't want her. Now that he could no longer use her in his bitter war against the McRaes, she was just a nuisance, an embarrassment. She was the woman who knew about his illness and his guilt-ridden nightmares... and about his real father.

She fell to her knees, curled into a ball and squeezed her eyes shut. Tears rolled onto her cheeks, her body shook with deep, wracking sobs. Never since her father died had she felt such intense, overwhelming pain. It squeezed her heart in a tight fist until she gasped for air. It churned and clawed at her insides, relentless, ripping her apart.

She had no idea how long she stayed there, prostrate on the floor and lost in darkness and grief.

The sudden hiss and crackle of logs collapsing on the fire grate forced her eyes open, and she remembered.

The medallion!

Pushed by an urge she didn't understand, she jumped to her feet, rushed to the fireplace and leant into the fire. Lodged between two logs, the medallion glowed as red as the flames, its leather tie already blackened and charred. It was far too hot for her to touch with her bare hands. Using the wrought-iron fire tongs, she lifted it off carefully, carried it across the room and dropped it into the washstand bowl. The water hissed, bubbled and a plume of steam rose in the air.

It would take a while to cool down. Lord McGunn didn't want it right now, but he might regret throwing it away one day and she would keep it safe for him. She looked around, her eyes widening when she spotted the jewellery pouch peeping through the opening of her tapestry bag. Of course. That could work.

An hour later, she sat on the bed in front of a glittering pile of necklaces and bangles. She selected a necklace, untied Bruce's medallion from its burnt leather tie and secured it to the chain amongst other baubles and charms. Holding the necklace out in front of her, she nodded with satisfaction. The medal was undetectable.

She slipped the necklace on but tidied the rest of the jewellery into the pouch. When she saw the wedding ring Cameron had given her and ordered not to wear before the ball, a fresh wave of anger and self-loathing washed over her and she tossed the ring across the room.

It bounced on the floor and rolled into a corner.

She had been fooled by Cameron. He was a liar and a cheat: she knew that now.

Her breath caught in her throat. What if he was more than that? The day before the so-called wedding, Malika claimed that he visited bordellos every night in Algiers, and that girls were afraid of him and his unpredictable, drunken moods. Rose had shouted that she was mean, petty and jealous and pushed her out of her room. But what if Malika had been right all along, and his behaviour during their wedding night hadn't been an aberration caused by too much champagne and her frigid response?

Her throat tightened as she recalled *that* night again. Cameron had rolled off the bed. Dishevelled, red and panting, and a snarl at the corner of his mouth, he had readjusted his breeches and yanked his shirt back on. 'What a silly girl you are to make so much fuss. You'll see, next time will be better, much better. I'll teach you to enjoy me, and to make me enjoy yourself more. I'll teach you all the things a good wife should know... For now, I'll leave you alone if you give me your father's diary. I want to read it again.'

When she had told him that the diary was in her mother's safe at the bank, he had become very pale, cursed loudly and stormed out of his suite. He had only returned at dawn to announce he was sailing back to Scotland on the *Sea Lady* right away. She was to keep her suite at the *Excelsior*, retrieve the diary and wait for his other clipper, the *Sea Eagle,* to arrive in Algiers and take her to Scotland. In the meantime she shouldn't wear her ring or tell anyone about the wedding, not even her mother, since he wanted to keep it a surprise until his birthday ball.

And she had been foolish enough to obey. She was indeed a stupid, stupid girl, and it was no wonder Bruce McGunn didn't want her.

Never had a night passed so slowly.

Rose lay in bed, exhausted but unable to sleep, desolate but unable to shed another tear. She watched shadows move on the walls, cast anxious glances towards the curtained window that made the room feel stifling like a tomb, and tried to block the burning memories of Bruce's kisses and caresses, and the agony caused by his rejection.

His teeth clenched so hard his jaw hurt, he curled his hand into a tight fist and punched the wall, once, then once again as he walked down the corridor. He punched so hard his knuckles bled, yet he felt nothing.

No, that wasn't true. He felt plenty. Self-loathing, despair, pain. And burning desire.

He yanked his boots off and threw them across the room. They fell on the wooden floorboards with a loud thud. Next he tugged his shirt out of his trousers, unfastened a couple of buttons and yanked it over his head before throwing it in a heap at the foot of the bed.

Hell. He could still taste her, smell her. He would never be able to get her scent out of his head ever again – that sweet, floral, woman scent that was uniquely hers, and that he was sure he'd crave for the rest of his days.

He had been so close to take her tonight. The moment he'd looked into her deep blue eyes, kissed her and felt her bare skin heat and shiver under his touch, his body had taken over.

Thankfully reality had jerked him back from the edge of the dark, hot precipice he was sliding into before it was too late. He had no right to her. No right at all. She was radiant, bursting with life and light whereas he was haunted by demons and the spectre of madness – and he'd just found out, the son of a murderer. Despite everything, he still had some remnants of a conscience.

She didn't want him anyway. She still hoped McRae would take her back. Well, that wasn't going to happen. Wallace would take her to his farm where she would stay, safe out of McRae's and Morven's reach.

He sat up on the bed, shoved a pillow behind his back and winced as his sore muscles and bruised ribs protested. Staring at the fire dancing in the hearth, he started replaying in his mind the events of the day.

What did Morven want with Rose? Was it really McNeil in the Nag's Head before or had he mistaken him for somebody else? Why did he think the same men who had ambushed him in Inverness were there tonight?

And the last, and most puzzling question. Was Donald Robertson his father?

As a matter of habit, he lifted his hand to his throat to toy with his medallion, before curling his fist and slamming it against the mattress. He had worn his mother's medallion since he was a baby. He had treasured it, felt for it at night when as a child he cried for the mother he would never know, and later as a good-luck charm before a dangerous mission.

He felt almost bereft now without it around his neck. However there was no way he'd ever wear something that had been obtained by murder and felony – and something that had once belonged to a McRae.

Chapter Eleven

'I'm glad to see you're up and ready, Miss Rose. I was just about to send for you.'

Wallace's voice behind her stopped her in her tracks. Bedbugs! Why was he here already, just as she was just about to try and talk the landlord into trading one of her silver necklaces for the loan of a horse and set off for Westmore.

She took a deep breath, forced a smile and turned to face him.

'Good morning, Mr Wallace.'

He didn't smile back. He looked serious, worried even.

'I'm afraid we must leave town as soon as possible. There's trouble at the harbour.'

'What kind of trouble?'

'A steamer has just docked to be loaded up with grain, the army cordoned off the area but I doubt they'll be able to hold people back very long.'

'Why would people want to hold them back?'

Wallace's face hardened. 'Because the people mean to prevent the steamer from being loaded up with grain.'

'I don't understand…'

'McRae keeps shipping tons of oats and barley to Newcastle, Liverpool or London when there's not enough to be sold to families here. People are fed up, Miss Rose. Fed up with starving or eating boiled grass and nettle soup. With the potato crop failing last year, things have gone from bad to worse – except for McRae, of course, who is lining his pockets when his people are suffering.'

Her chest tightened. How could she ever have believed Cameron innocent of all the wrong-doings and the suffering on his estate, and believe it was Morven, and Morven alone, who was responsible?

Shivering despite her thick cloak, she followed Wallace into the courtyard where a brown mare and a grey horse were being saddled, their breath steaming in the cold, grey foggy morning.

Wallace pointed out to the mare.

'This one's yours. Lieutenant McGunn bought it for you before he left. He was in a great hurry to be on his way.' He cast her a quizzical glance. 'So much in a hurry I'm afraid he didn't have time to bid you goodbye.'

'That's all right,' she retorted with as much indifference as she could muster, 'I know the man to be totally devoid of social graces and wasn't expecting him to.'

That was a lie. It had stung to stand at her window to watch his tall, black-clad figure ride to the end the street then disappear, swallowed up by the freezing fog, and to realise he cared so little about her he hadn't even bothered to bid her goodbye.

Wallace smiled. 'Aye, Miss Rose. It's true he was never one to mince his words or waste time with niceties, but you couldn't find a more true and loyal friend, and that's what counts in the end, isn't it?'

Feeling chastised she bent her head and sighed. 'I suppose so.'

He held out his hand. 'Here, let me take your bag and strap it to the saddle.'

He helped her climb up and they rode out of the courtyard and into a dense crowd. The silence was intense, almost deafening and anything but peaceful, she thought as she urged her horse into a walking pace and followed Wallace.

They were about half way up the main street when a series of gunshots ripped through the morning like thunder, startling Rose's horse. Screaming erupted around her. The crowd moved back and forth like a giant wave, making it hard for her to rein the horse in and stop it from trampling over the people around her.

Emerging from the fog like a ghostly army, soldiers marched towards the square, their bayonets pointing forward, whereas at the other end of the square at least two dozen special constables ran up the street, waving their truncheons and hitting anybody standing in their path.

Fear made Rose's heart pound. Bile rose in her throat. It was hopeless! Why didn't these people run away? Couldn't they see they were trapped and risked getting shot, stabbed or crushed to death?

Her horse snorted and started to rear. She gripped the reins so tightly her knuckles went white. Looking around in a panic, she saw that the crowd's movements were pushing Wallace towards the soldiers, further away from her.

'Get away, Miss Rose,' he shouted. 'Head towards the church. At the crossroads take the coast road towards Melvich. There's an inn, The Valiant Stag at the edge of town. I'll meet you there.'

He said something else but his words were drowned in the clamour of the crowd.

She urged her horse forward and manoeuvred through the crowd inch by inch. Next to her a constable, his face contorted in anger, brought down his club onto a woman's back, deaf to her pleas for mercy and the shrieks of the little girl who clung to her blood-splattered skirt. When the woman collapsed to the ground, he started kicking her with his black hob-nailed boots.

'Stop! Are you mad? You're going to kill her,' Rose shouted, but he ignored her and gave the woman one last ferocious kick before aiming his club at the little girl.

With a howl of rage, Rose pushed her horse straight into him. He lost his balance and fell on the cobbles. Then everything then went too fast. She tried to haul back on the reins but her horse was out of control. As she struggled to stay on the saddle she heard the constable scream as he was crushed under her horse's hooves.

After felt like hours she managed to push her way out of the square and into a quieter back street. Breathless, her hands shaking so badly she could hardly hold on to the reins, she leant to one side. Tears streamed down her face as she heaved, gagged and coughed until her stomach was empty.

Wiping her mouth with a corner of her cloak, she sat up and looked around. A church steeple rose above the slate rooftops. If she rode that way, she would end up on the road to Melvich. She started the mare in the opposite direction. She wasn't going to Melvich. She was going to Westmore.

The morning fog had cleared by the time Bruce rode past Westmore's imposing gates. He took note of the two pretentious stone griffins, heraldic symbols of the McRaes', which now towered from the gateposts. They hadn't been there when he came to Westmore with his grandfather – his only ever visit. He was ten.

He'd often wondered what had prompted Doughall McGunn to visit Westmore that time. He had no idea what had taken place between him and Lady Patricia, but his grandfather hadn't sobered up for a whole week on his return to Wrath and had embarked on a series of costly improvements to the fisheries shortly after.

He remembered every detail of that short visit – being fed soup and buttered scones in the kitchen while his grandfather had his interview with Lady Patricia, being shooed outside by an impatient butler dressed in parrot green, red and gold. He had time to explore the fancy grounds, find a pond to throw stones into and a couple of trees to climb before his grandfather had shouted that it was time to leave. He hadn't set foot in the castle, or met with young McRae or his mother then.

He hadn't thought about it for years. Funny how it was all coming back now.

He took a deep breath. Never mind childhood memories. He needed to focus on what he would tell McRae if he was to save Wrath from his and his unscrupulous bankers' greed.

He rode up the two-mile lane leading to the manor house. Perched on top of a small hill, it favoured a French chateau with its turrets, spires and chimneys, and the white walls that glowed in the dull winter light. Elaborate topiaries and statues of Greek and Roman gods scattered manicured parterres. Fountains spurted water towards the grey skies. Lady Patricia and her son had spared no expense to make Westmore one of the grandest manor houses in the whole of Scotland.

Once inside the courtyard he signalled to a stable boy and ordered him to watch his horse.

'Give him some oats and water,' he instructed before jumping down and slipping the lad a coin. He didn't plan to stay long, so it wasn't necessary to take his saddle bags with him.

Around him an army of servants dressed in the same garish livery he remembered unloaded carts and carriages and rushed through service doors, their arms filled with extravagant bouquets, bottles of wine and spirits, and crates filled with fresh produce and exotic fruit, among which he recognised mangoes, pineapples, oranges and pomelos.

He decided against following them and instead walked around to the main entrance. A butler wearing a starchy expression contrasting sorely with his colourful clothing, opened the door, eyed him suspiciously and showed him in after he introduced himself.

Damn, he thought as he waited in the gigantic hall. Westmore was truly a palace fit for a king. The hallway's chequered black and white floor gleamed under the glittering lights of several enormous crystal chandeliers. Huge paintings, mostly hunting scenes and landscapes, adorned the walls. The contrast with Wrath's dusty hunting trophies, chipped stone flags and threadbare curtains couldn't be starker.

'His Lordship will see my lord in the library,' the butler called when he came back. 'If my lord would care to follow me.'

Bruce smiled as he caught a glimpse of his reflection in a tall gilded mirror as they left the hall. No wonder the man looked down at him. With his long, dark hair and stubbly cheeks, and the cuts and bruises on his face, not to mention his muddy coat and riding boots, ripped jacket and crumpled white shirt, he belonged more to a seedy backstreet tavern than a palace like Westmore.

He followed the butler along endless corridors, past a succession of richly furnished drawing rooms, a banqueting suite and a ballroom where crystal chandeliers dripped from moulded ceilings, their lights reflecting onto the polished parquet flooring. In every room gold brocade curtains draped tall windows and gilded griffins adorned enormous mantelpieces. Everywhere servants dusted furniture, polished already gleaming mirrors and floors, and arranged elaborate flower displays. The whole castle buzzed with the preparations for McRae's grand ball.

At last the butler opened a door to the library. Bruce paused in the doorway and blinked. Light poured in through large French windows which opened onto a terrace and offered a breathtaking view of the grounds and of the dull, slate grey waters of the Firth in the distance. Every wall but one was lined with bookshelves from floor to ceiling – the remaining wall being covered with portraits.

Leather armchairs and lacquered Chinese cabinets were scattered around the room, but unlike his own desk at Wrath, McRae's walnut kneehole desk was free of clutter and sported a silver inkwell, a rosewood cigar box and an oil lamp.

Once the butler had closed the door behind him, Bruce strode across the room to take a look at the collection of portraits, most of them of men in sombre black attire, hunting outfit or parade uniforms posing proudly for posterity. As he scanned through the paintings, his eyes were attracted by one of the smaller portraits and he stepped a little closer.

There was something familiar about the tall, powerfully built man wearing the scarlet coat, dark green tartan kilt, white and red diced hose of the 92nd Gordon Highlanders. He was of course familiar with the uniform, since he too had worn it until his discharge eighteen months before. The man in the painting had one hand resting on the pommel of his claymore, while he held his blue bonnet topped with six black ostrich feathers with the other.

Niall McRae. It had to be him. In the right-hand corner of the painting were the artist's signature and a date: April 1815. This must be Niall McRae's last painting before Quatre-Bras. Less than two months later, he would be dead.

He looked more closely at the man's face. It was like staring at his own reflection. Damn, he must be more tired than he thought. He was seeing things. Niall McRae was indeed tall and dark-haired, but he looked nothing like him. It was the uniform, and the light playing tricks on him, that was all.

He made himself focus on the medals pinned on the man's broad chest: the Egyptian sphinx, the 1813 Vittoria gold medal, and one half of the medal of the battle of Alexandria. After listening to Rose reading her father's journal, he had expected to see it there. Only there was something odd, he thought as he leant closer. The artist appeared to have painted the wrong half of the medal.

He shrugged. It was probably only a mirror effect, and in any case, it didn't really matter which half McRae was wearing. Did it?

Of course it bloody well did! Actually there was a way to find out which half McRae wore in the painting, and it was to decipher the two numbers engraved on the medal. Bruce narrowed his eyes, tried different angles and stifled another curse. It was no good. The numbers were too small. He needed a magnifying glass. He turned round, his gaze skimmed the room, stopped at McRae's desk.

He was half way across the room when the door opened and McRae walked in.

They both froze and stared at each other. They hadn't met since the enquiry at Whitehall eighteen months before, when McRae had accompanied his friend Frazier to a couple of hearings.

Bruce swallowed hard, remembering all too well McRae's mocking looks and sneering comments as his actions were being scrutinized and his future played out.

Dressed in light grey, tight-fitting trousers, maroon tailcoat and a pink and almond green silk waistcoat, MacRae was as usual the epitome of wealth and elegance. Bruce took a deep breath. He may be a dandy, but he was also the man who was trying to ruin him, the man who had lied to Rose, made a fool of her – his throat tightened – the man who'd seduced her.

'This is an unexpected pleasure, McGunn.' An uneasy smile flickered on McRae's lips – or was it a nervous twitch? 'I thought my butler had gone raving mad or had supped too much liquor when he announced you were here.'

McGunn bowed his head in a curt greeting.

'McRae.'

As McRae came closer, Bruce noticed his pasty face, the purple shadows under his eyes and the traces of liquor and cigar smoke emanating from his person. The man's dissolute lifestyle must be catching up with him.

'You look as if you encountered some kind of… problem on your way here, McGunn. I hope your injuries aren't too painful.'

Of course, he must already know about the beating at the harbour the night before. No doubt Morven's thugs had already made their report.

'It's nothing for you to worry about,' Bruce replied with feigned indifference, even if at that moment he wanted nothing more than wipe the smirk of McRae's face.

'Very well. Please sit down.'

McRae gestured towards an armchair and sat behind the kneehole desk. He may look calm, languid even, but the nervous glance he darted towards the family portraits did not escape Bruce's attention, and neither did the trembling of his hand as he opened the rosewood cigar box and held it out for Bruce to help himself. When Bruce declined, he dug a cigar out and stuck it between his teeth.

'You don't smoke? Too bad. These Partagás are imported from Havana especially for me.'

He lit the cigar, and took a few deep, long puffs.

'So tell me, what can I do for you? I take it you're not here to wish me a happy birthday or congratulate me on my engagement to Lady Sophia.'

'It would be rude of me not to,' Bruce said. 'Many happy returns, and my best wishes to you and your fiancée.'

McRae nodded. 'Thank you. By the way, where is your travelling companion?'

'Miss Saintclair?' Bruce asked, nonchalant. 'What about her?'

'Is she here with you?' The twitch at the side of McRae's mouth became more pronounced.

Was he afraid of Rose waiting for the chance to ruin the ball and his engagement Lady Sophia, or was he only thinking about Colonel Saintclair's diary?

'No, she's not here,' he replied after a short silence.

McRae flicked ash off his cigar into a silver ashtray and added, his voice unsteady.

'Ah… May I ask where she is?'

'I left her in Porthaven this morning. As far as I know, she's still there,' Bruce lied. By now he fully expected the young woman to be safely tucked away on Wallace's farm, out of reach of Morven and his gang.

'The thing is, Miss Saintclair has something my mother is most anxious to see, something she was bringing from Algiers especially for her.'

'Does she now? And what would it be?'

McRae tapped his cigar against the side of the ashtray.

'She didn't tell you anything?'

'I am afraid I have no idea what you are talking about, McRae.'

The man squirmed in his seat, and Bruce was enjoying every second of it. It was obvious he wondered how much Bruce knew about the fake wedding and the journal. It was a damned shame Bruce couldn't use Rose's pretend wedding as a lever to against McRae's bankers. He had thought about it, but without any proof that it had ever taken place it would be Rose's word against McRae's. What was more, he was reluctant to expose the young woman to public scrutiny.

McRae drew on his cigar and his face soon disappeared behind a cloud of smoke. An uneasy silence descended between them, a silence that Bruce had no intention of breaking.

At last, McRae leant over the desk.

'Why are you here, McGunn?'

Bruce stared him straight in the eye.

'I have a business proposal for you. About Wrath and the bank loans.'

McRae cocked his head to one side, his lips stretched into a conceited smile and he let out a long sigh.

'At last you realised you have no alternative than to sell Wrath to me. That's excellent news, excellent news indeed.'

Bruce opened his mouth to say that hell would freeze over before he sold him even a handful of McGunn soil and was about to inform him that the *Sea Eagle* was being held to ransom at Wrath when McRae added.

'My lawyers, Langford and Stewart, happen to be here, putting the final touches to my marriage contract. I'm sure they can have the preliminary sales agreement drawn up in no time.'

Langford and Stewart were the lawyers Colonel Saintclair wrote to about Niall McRae's last will and testament, the ones Pichet had met in Inverness before getting himself killed, and the men who knew about that mysterious third letter…

He glanced at Niall McRae's portrait and his breath grew short. Suddenly it was vital that he stay at Westmore to look at the painting again and talk to the lawyers. For that he needed to change his plans and pretend he wanted to sell Wrath.

'I want it to be clear that I'm not agreeing to anything until I see your lawyers' proposal,' he said, rising to his feet.

'Of course.'

McRae stubbed the end of his cigar in a silver ashtray and stood up too.

'Please attend the ball tonight and be my honoured guest until the lawyers produce a draft sales agreement. I can't wait to tell everybody the news. It's not every day a McGunn bows down to a McRae.'

He laughed again. 'In fact, I don't believe it ever happened before.'

Bruce curled his fist by his side, striving to repress the urge of smashing it into the man's pasty face and swallowed hard. He would bow to no man, and certainly not to a McRae. Yet he had to let the McRae believe he had won for now.

'No one is to know until I agree to the proposal,' he cut in sharply. 'You only tell your bankers and the lawyers, or the sale is off. Is that clear?'

McRae chuckled. 'Oh, very well if you insist. Shall we toast to our agreement? I have an excellent Fine Napoleon cognac.'

'No, thank you. It would be a little premature.' He paused. 'Actually, there was something else I needed to talk to you about. Two bodies were washed up on my beaches earlier this week – two women, one of whom Rose Saintclair identified as her best friend Malika Jahal.'

He watched McRae closely for a reaction. There was none. The man's eyes didn't show a flicker of emotion, regret or even surprise. Rose would have been disappointed. Contrary to what she thought, the man wasn't in the least overwhelmed by the news.

'Malika, dead?' he said at last. 'How very sad. She left Westmore about ten days ago. Rumour has it she ran off to Inverness. Actually, that would have been at around the same time you were there, wouldn't it? Maybe you met her there...'

Bruce's stomach knotted. Why did McRae mention his visit to Inverness? Images of Malika flashed before his eyes. Malika alive and scared, barely dressed, in a large brass bed. Malika's dead, empty eyes staring at the grey sky on the beach.

'Why would I?' He forced the words out. 'Anyway, Miss Saintclair is understandably very upset, and very surprised too, since her friend never mentioned her intention of travelling to Scotland on the *Sea Lady*.'

He stared at MacRae. 'I assume she travelled on the *Sea Lady*.'

'Indeed. She was planning a surprise reunion here with Miss Saintclair,' McRae replied. 'Apparently the two young ladies had argued and Malika felt remorseful.'

'Then why did she leave Westmore before Miss Saintclair arrived?'

McRae shrugged and looked away. 'Who knows? She was a volatile, headstrong young woman. To tell you the truth, she and I didn't really get on.'

This time McRae looked uncomfortable. Something wasn't right, but Bruce couldn't quite point out what.

'So you have no idea why she left Westmore and what happened to her?'

'None whatsoever. Have you?'

Bruce stiffened. 'Of course not. I didn't even know the woman.'

McRae opened the door and the two men walked out of the library.

'Of course, how silly of me...'

Once again Bruce has the uneasy feeling that McRae knew something he didn't, and he didn't like it one bit.

'Perhaps I could question the dancers and musicians,' he suggested.

This time, McRae laughed.

'You're welcome to try, but they only speak Arabic, and a few words of French. They will be performing here tonight, so you can try and speak to them then. Anyway, I must leave you now. As you can imagine I still have a lot to organise for the ball.'

'Baxter will take you to your room now. He'll sort out a suit for you and everything you might need for tonight. Please make yourself at home.'

There was little chance of that, Bruce thought as he watched him walk down the corridor. He glanced back at the library door with a stab of regret. He would have to come back later to take a closer look at Niall McRae's portrait, when the ball was in full swing and everybody was too busy enjoying themselves dancing to McRae's string orchestra, eating his canapés and drinking his champagne to pay him any attention.

Chapter Twelve

Rose didn't see the pothole until it was too late. The mare stumbled straight into it, almost throwing her to the ground and into a large puddle filled with mud and partly melted snow.

'There, there, that's a good girl…'

She patted the horse's neck with a shaky hand and issued soothing words. It wouldn't be able to carry on much further, it was exhausted. So was she, but it was no excuse. She should have been paying more attention to the road.

She dismounted and started walking on the uneven track, leading the horse behind her. Where was she? She should have reached Westmore by now. The light grew dim and blue, shadows thickened and closed in on her. She pulled the sides of her cloak more tightly as the sea breeze blew colder. If she didn't find Westmore or some kind of shelter before nightfall, she would be in serious trouble.

Not for the first time since riding out of Porthaven that morning, doubt gnawed at her. Perhaps she'd been wrong to leave Wallace behind and come here alone: it might have been safer to go to his farm and wait there for Lord McGunn. She'd had to turn back on herself several times since the morning, and now it looked like she'd taken the wrong road once again.

Then she spotted the stone figures that stood on top of the high stone wall running alongside the track and her heart beat faster – half lion half bird. Griffins! So she had reached Westmore at last.

Now all she had to do was find the main entrance, slip into the park unnoticed by the gatekeeper and make her way to the hunting lodge where she planned to talk to the dancers and musicians. This time luck was on her side. Just as darkness stifled the last glimmers of daylight, she came across a small opening in the wall with a wrought-iron gate flapping in the wind with a squeaky noise.

Still pulling the mare behind her, she pushed the gate open and started onto a lane winding its way between the trees and their wide, sweeping branches. The snow had melted in patches and her feet crushed a thick carpet of pine needles, releasing a scent so strong it was as if Bruce were here, right next to her.

She swayed against the horse and leant against its comforting warmth. Where was *he* this evening? Probably on his way to Wallace's farm. He could hardly stay at Westmore after issuing threats to destroy the *Sea Eagle*. She didn't want to think about the way he'd react when he found out that she wasn't there. Would he worry that she'd been hurt in the riots and look for her in Porthaven, or would he guess that she'd come here despite his instructions?

She let out a long sigh. Suddenly it wasn't just doubt, but guilt as well, niggling at her. Well, it was too late for either. She was here now, ready to confront Cameron about his lies. Strange how it didn't seem so important now she realised she did not love the man, and probably never had. What was important, though, was to find out what had happened to Malika…

She tossed her head back, gave the reins a sharp pull, and walked out of the woods.

The sight of the castle made her draw breath in awe.

With its tall spires and dozens of towers darting towards the sky, with fountains and statues lit by coloured lanterns and the main road lined with blazing torches, it looked like a fairytale castle…and a far cry indeed from Wrath Lodge.

She followed the lane towards another copse. Soon lights glowed through the trees and the outline of a large two-storey stone house appeared. As she got nearer, echoes of a music she recognised only too well drifted towards her – the high-pitched *gisba* flute, accompanied by the dull rhythms of *bendir* drum and melodious chords of a *luth*. Suddenly she wasn't in the far North of Scotland anymore, but home in Bou Saada.

She approached the house with caution, but there were no guards at the front door. Just to be on the safe side, however,

142

she tiptoed around the back. After tying the mare to a post, she paused to listen to the music again. It came from one of the downstairs rooms.

Creeping close to the window, she peered inside. The three musicians she remembered from Algiers sat on large cushions on the floor. They were alone. Rose tapped on the glass, and the *luth* player turned to her. His eyes opened wide in shock. He dropped instrument to the floor, jumped to his feet, and ran to the window.

He lifted the window sash up and leant out.

'*Ourida? hl htha hqyqi?*'

She couldn't help but smile. It was good to hear her name in Arabic, *Ourida*, 'Little Rose' – the name her father, family and friends called her back at home.

'*Salaem'alekoum.*' She bowed her head. 'Yes, it's me, and no, you're not dreaming,' she whispered in Arabic.

'*Wa'alekoum salaam,*' the musician replied, bowing in return, his greeting echoed by his companions who had rushed to his side.

When she raised her hand to silence their questions, she wasn't smiling anymore. 'I need your help, my friends.'

'My clerks will work on the documents tonight, my Lord, and I'll have a draft agreement ready by tomorrow,' Charles Longford gathered a pile of papers into a black leather portfolio before rising to his feet.

'That soon?'

Two faint pink spots appeared on the old man's cheeks and there was a flicker of unease in his pale blue eyes.

'With all due respect, my Lord, we have been preparing for this eventuality for a while.'

Bruce narrowed his eyes.

'You have?'

'Well, it's no secret that your estate is in a delicate financial situation and that you are not in the best of health…'

This time Bruce had to make a conscious effort to retain his calm.

'I had no idea my health – or lack of – was worth gossiping about.'

The lawyer had the decency to look embarrassed. He coughed to clear his throat, smoothed his thinning grey hair with a shaky hand and tucked the portfolio under his arm.

'I can assure you that my associate and I do not gossip,' he replied stiffly.

Bruce walked to the window. He had been given a room on the second floor at the front of the castle with a good view of the grounds and of the stream of elegant carriages that queued in front of the porch steps, waiting to disgorge their well-dressed, perfumed and bejewelled occupants.

He had bathed and shaved, and now wore his spare black jacket, trousers and a crisp white shirt a maidservant had pressed for him. His lip curled as he looked at his reflection in the window. If it weren't for his hair, far too long for the prevailing fashion, and the cuts and bruises on his face, he could almost pass for one of McRae's cronies.

He turned to face Charles Langford and crossed his arms on his chest.

'Enlighten me, Langford, what exactly is wrong with my health?'

The two pink spots on the man's cheeks deepened to dark red. He coughed again.

'We heard my lord suffered from… I mean, there have been rumours that my lord was afflicted with…' He paused, drew in a deep breath. '…an incurable illness.'

Bruce arched his eyebrows.

'Is that so? And you carried draft sales documents with you just in case I happened to stop by at Westmore before I dropped dead?'

Looking even more agitated, the lawyer shook his head.

'No. Of course not. My associate and I were going to travel to Wrath this very week to put to you a purchase offer from Lord McRae. Your coming here today saves us a long and uncomfortable journey.'

'I'm glad to oblige,' Bruce replied pleasantly, but inside he was seething.

144

Someone from Wrath had talked. Someone who knew about his debilitating memory losses, his headaches and the nightmares that had these past few months kept him from sleeping at night – someone who had noticed his slow descent into insanity. Who could it be?

However infuriating, there was no time to dig deeper right now.

'Will that be all, my lord?' Charles Langford looked at him in earnest.

'What do you remember about a French officer, a man named Pichet who paid you a visit about Niall McRae in August 1815?' Bruce asked abruptly.

He had intended to take the man by surprise. He had succeeded.

Charles Langford's face drained of all colour, his mouth opened on a silent gasp, and panic flickered in his eyes. The portfolio slipped from his grasp and fell on the floor with a loud noise.

'Well?' Bruce asked again.

The old man bent down and picked up the leather wallet with trembling fingers.

'Thirty years ago? I am sorry, I don't recall ever meeting this gentleman.'

Bruce stared at him. He was lying. The question was why.

'The McRaes being your most important clients, I would expect you to remember everything about them, especially something as unusual as Pichet's visit.'

The old man closed his eyes briefly.

'Pichet, you said? Now that you mention it, I do vaguely recall a Frenchman visiting our offices.'

'What do you remember about him?'

Langford shook his head.

'I am afraid my memory is hazy. I shall have to confer with my associate – it was a long time ago.'

'Nonsense. There's nothing wrong with your memory! You just gave me a list of most of my assets without even reading your notes, so surely you can remember the Frenchman who brought you Niall McRae's last will and testament.'

Bruce walked towards him. Langford stepped back, a terrified look in his watery blue eyes. Damn it, did the old man think he was going to hit him?

'How do you know about that?'

'Let's say I came upon some papers – some very interesting papers. So what changes did the new will make to McRae's succession?'

'You must realise I cannot discuss any confidential matters regarding the McRae family affairs with you or anyone not related...' he coughed, and spoke the rest of the sentence so fast his words seemed to stumble over one another, 'not related to the family of the deceased, my lord.'

Bruce shrugged, impatient. 'I know Pichet was carrying three letters. One for you, one for Lady Patricia. Did he tell you about the third letter?'

His hand clutching the portfolio tightly, the old man took another step back towards the door.

'I don't recall the man Pichet mentioning another letter, my lord.'

It was plain Langford wasn't going to say anything more. Bruce took a deep breath. He had to try something else.

'It must have been very upsetting for Lady Patricia to receive her husband's letter as well as his personal items – his flask, tobacco case and gloves, and I believe an embroidered handkerchief... Anything else?'

The old man's shoulders seemed to lose their stiffness and he let out a shaky breath. He must have thought he'd better answer at least some of Bruce's queries because he was more accommodating suddenly.

'Once again, I fail to understand how you can be in possession of such detailed personal information, sir, but...ahem...you are right. Monsieur Pichet did entrust me with Lord Niall's letter and personal effects, which I took to Westmore. There wasn't much, just the items you mentioned.'

'Nothing else, you are quite sure?' Bruce frowned, pensive. So the medallion wasn't destined to Lady Patricia.

'Positive. I will never forget how upset poor Lady Patricia was to receive her husband's monogrammed handkerchief, stained with his own blood. It was part of a set she had embroidered herself and given him as a wedding present, only six months before.'

This time, Bruce's heart flipped in his chest. 'They'd been married only six months?'

'That's right, they were married in March 1815, only a couple of months before Lord McRae's regiment was dispatched to Belgium. It was a terrible ordeal for her, in her…ahem… delicate condition.'

'What delicate condition?' Bruce repeated without understanding.

Charles Langford nodded. 'At the end of August, she was only half-way through her pregnancy of course. It was all very, very sad…'

It suddenly hit him. Of course! What a fool he'd been not to see what had been staring him in the face all along. Niall McRae was desperate to provide for his son and the woman he loved, but Cameron wasn't born then, and that could only mean one thing. The son he was referring to wasn't Cameron, and the woman he so wanted to protect and care for wasn't Lady Patricia.

That was why Langford hadn't mentioned the half medal. McRae didn't send it to Lady Patricia, but to that other woman – the mother of his son, and the woman he loved – together with the third letter.

No wonder Lady Patricia was so eager to get her hands on Colonel Saintclair's diary, and Cameron was ready to go to any length to acquire, and destroy it. What Colonel Saintclair had written in his diary changed everything.

He remembered Niall McRae's portrait in the library – a tall, broad-shouldered, dark-haired man. His throat tightened and he suddenly found it hard to breathe. Could it be that…?

'Will that be all, my Lord?' Charles Langford stared at him, an inquisitive look in his blue eyes.

'Yes, Langford, that will be all,' he answered absent-mindedly. 'Thank you.'

He had some thinking to do, all he wanted now was to be alone. He hardly noticed when the old man bowed and let himself out.

'What do you think of the party so far? It's rather splendid, isn't it?'

McRae handed him a champagne flute. Bruce drank a sip and winced. He didn't care much for fizzy wine at the best of times, but that one left a foul taste in his mouth.

He surveyed the ballroom, magnificent with its crystal chandeliers, gilded wall mirrors and shiny parquet flooring and the couples dancing to the orchestra's waltzes, cotillons and quadrilles. There had been rousing polkas and mazurkas, the latest dance crazes to sweep across the ballrooms of Europe, or so an elderly gentleman had informed him a few moments before.

Women, dressed in delicate pastels or deep, shimmering blues or crimsons, swirled past on the arm of their dance companions, their jewellery dazzling under the lights.

'Aye, it's very impressive,' he replied at last, turning to look at his host.

They were the same height, McRae a slighter built, probably because he'd never had to train hard or fight. Nevertheless Bruce had to admit the man cut a dashing figure in a sober black suit, his shirt and silk cravat gleaming white against the dark wool, and shiny gold-coloured buttons shaped like griffins adorning its jacket.

It was no wonder he had dazzled a naive young woman like Rose. In fact he must have looked like a fairytale prince charming, the man every little girl dreamt of. Watching McRae earlier on as he paraded in the ballroom's extravagant decor as if he didn't have a care in the world was enough for Bruce to feel the urge to smash his fist in his face all over again.

If Bruce didn't like the champagne, McRae seemed to have no problem draining his flute, and from the unnatural glow in his blue eyes and the animated tone of his voice, it was clear that it wasn't his first either. He leant towards Bruce in a conspiratorial manner.

'I daresay it will soon get even better. I have a surprise for my guests – my male guests, that is – I think all will enjoy. I guarantee it'll cheer you up.'

Bruce arched one eyebrow. 'Then I'll look forward to your surprise, McRae.'

He surveyed the room. 'I don't see Lady Patricia.'

Cameron's face clouded over. He plucked another flute from the tray of a passing waiter.

'My mother has been taken ill and will unfortunately not be joining us tonight.'

He drank more champagne and turned to watch a couple twirling on the dance floor to the lively tune of a polka. The woman, tall and rake thin, was dressed in a pale and unflattering shade of blue. Her dance partner wore the 9nd Gordon Highlanders officer's parade uniform.

'Ah, here she is – my lovely fiancée, dancing with someone I think you are well acquainted with.'

Bruce's shoulders stiffened. There was a man he had hoped never to meet again.

'Captain Frazier.' His fingers tightening around the stem of the flute, he watched the couple dance.

The last time he'd seen him was at the Whitehall enquiry when Frazier was cleared of all wrongdoing and Bruce discharged for misconduct. That had been their first encounter since the man had run away from the battlefield at Ferozeshah, allegedly suffering from heatstroke and leaving Bruce's men and himself exposed to enemy fire – and the deadly explosion of the ammunition depot.

A dull ache now throbbed on his temple, just above his right eye. He felt himself grow a little shaky, and the bright lights suddenly hurt his eyes. Damn. This wasn't a good time to suffer another fit.

He'd better get a grip on himself, the last thing he wanted was for McRae and Frazier to notice he was unwell. There were clearly enough rumours flying about as it was. He took a long, deep, calming breath, put his half-drunk flute down on a console, and focussed on the dancing couple.

Lady Sophia's lacklustre brown hair was curled in tight ringlets and bounced around her slim face, her eyes were narrowed to slits and her lips pinched in concentration as she followed the dance steps. Frazier hadn't changed in the year and a half since he'd last seen him. With his blond hair flopping fashionably on his high forehead and a gormless smile plastered on his fleshy lips, he seemed not to have a care in the world.

And why would he not be enjoying himself? Bruce sneered. He wasn't the man who got discharged and was now fighting to save his estate and his people – the man who was slowly, inexorably, going mad.

'My dear,' McRae held out his hand to his fiancée when the polka had finished, 'let me introduce you to Lord McGunn who is paying us an unexpected visit.'

The woman's small brown eyes opened wide in shock and she recoiled as if faced with a dangerous animal. Bruce bowed as Lady Sophia recovered her manners. She muttered a greeting and curtsied quickly. Next to her, Frazier blushed a deep crimson.

'Lieutenant McGunn... I never thought... ah... I'd see you here,' he stammered.

Bruce nodded curtly. 'Frazier.'

'I hope you are... ah ... well,' the man added, his fingers fiddling restless, with the tie of his red and yellow sash.

'Why wouldn't I be?'

There was a short, uncomfortable silence. Frazier cleared his throat as if to speak but didn't seem to find anything to say. Bruce would be damned if he made it easier for him. What lay between them was more than mere enmity and wounded pride – it was the blood of many good men.

'I don't know about you, my dear girl,' McRae said, slipping his arm under Lady Sophia's arm, 'but I'm in great need of a bowl of punch.'

She nodded in agreement, and McRae turned to Frazier. 'Would you care to join us?'

'Of course,' Frazier nodded, hardly able hide his relief.

Bruce watched as the trio made their way through the crowd and out of the ballroom, then turned on his heel and walked out through a door at the opposite end. Hopefully people were too engrossed in the music, the dance, the buffet or the gossips, to notice him as he slipped into the library.

His heart beat a little too fast as he closed the door behind him. Slightly dizzy, he leaned against the door panel. The room was empty and dark except for a single oil lamp on the desk that gave a little light.

He closed his eyes, and waited for his heartbeat to return to normal.

This was madness.

What exactly was he hoping to find? Some kind of proof that the farfetched notion that had taken shape in his mind after his conversation with Charles Langford was indeed based on truth? The fantasy that Niall McRae might be his…

No, this was ludicrous! He almost opened the door and walked out again when something stopped him. It wasn't quite the sound of a woman's voice, or the touch of a woman's hand against his cheek. It was like a gentle whispering wind enveloping him, coaxing him, urging him to go to Niall McRae's portrait, and lift it off the wall.

He carried it with great care to the desk, pushed the lamp closer and turned it up to get more light. His breath short, he searched through the drawers for a magnifying glass, found one and bent down over the painting to read the inscription.

The sound the magnifying glass made when he dropped it on the desk echoed in the library. So he'd been right. The Battle of Alexandria had taken place in 1801, his medal had borne the first two digits, 18. McRae wore the other half of the Battle of Alexandria medal, the one that read 01.

He made himself check again.

Was he reading too much into the portrait? Could it be that the artist made a simple mistake, and that the fact Niall McRae looked like him was a mere coincidence?

He stared at the man in the painting, his dark hair, his proud stance, his uniform – and the claymore at his side. No, there was more than a mere resemblance. If McRae's hair had been shorter, he could be McGunn himself.

A long-forgotten event pushed its way into his memory. He had once called in the regimental mess where a reunion of officers who had fought at Quatre-Bras and Waterloo was underway. An old man – a colonel, judging by his uniform – had stared at him across the room most of the evening with rheumy blue eyes. Sometime after the toasts he had ambled towards him, gripped his arm in a claw-like vice, and asked his name. 'Lieutenant McGunn?' he had repeated, disappointment in his voice as if he was hoping to hear another name. 'Sorry, man, you reminded me of someone I used to know a long time ago. Damn strange how you look like the man too. Thought you might have been his son. The poor chap died at Quatre-Bras.'

Bruce had dismissed the event as delusions of an old man who'd drunk too much whisky. He hadn't thought about it for a long time. Of course, it now took a completely different meaning. It was obvious who the old man was thinking of. Niall McRae.

His father.

The light grew dimmer, the room shrank, closed in on him, and the world as he knew it collapsed.

Rose and Bruce's story concludes in

Sword Dance

Book 3 of the Dancing for the Devil Trilogy, available in March 2016.

For more information about **Marie Laval**

and other **Accent Press** titles

please visit

www.accentpress.co.uk

Lightning Source UK Ltd.
Milton Keynes UK
UKOW01f2317310316

271239UK00001B/14/P